MW00940609

Treasure in Sugar's Book Barn

A Bailey Fish Adventure

Linda Salisbury

Drawings by Carol Tornatore

Tabby House

Cover design and illustrations: Carol Tornatore
Author photo: Elaine Taylor

ISBN-13: 978-1-881539-49-0

ISBN-10: 1-881539-49-0

Library of Congress Control Number: 2010909420

Manufactured within CPSIA guidelines.
Printed by Sheridan Books, Inc.
Ann Arbor, Michigan
10/18/2010
Batch #1

baileyfish@gmail.com
www.BaileyFishAdventures.com
www.BaileyFishAdventureBooks.blogspot/com
Facebook: Author Linda Salisbury

Classroom quantities and *Teacher's Guides* available.

Tabby House
P.O. Box 544, Mineral, VA 23117
(540) 895-9093

Contents

1

Boxes

Bailey Fish yelped when she stubbed her big toe on a large box in the hall near her grandmother's library.

"Yikes! That hurts!" Bailey exclaimed, hopping on her left foot. The box hadn't been there in the morning when Bailey left for school. She stumbled to her grandmother's recliner and studied her big toe. It was bleeding just a little around the nail. She heard the screen door to the back porch *whap* shut.

"Bailey, are you home?" called her grandmother from the kitchen.

"In the library, Sugar," Bailey called back.

"Could you give me a hand? I have lots to unload from the truck." The door *whapped* again.

Bailey's toe was sore. "Sure," said Bailey, gingerly stepping on her right foot. She limped to the kitchen and out the door. Her grandmother stood next to her red pickup. Bailey could see that the truck bed was piled high with large cardboard boxes. Her curiosity made her forget about her throbbing toe.

"What's all that?" Bailey asked. She never knew what Sugar would bring home from thrift stores or yard sales where her grandmother always looked for bargains. *Maybe she found more treasures,* thought Bailey.

"It's part of a surprise for later. There are so many boxes that I need your help carrying them inside," said Sugar.

"Wow! They're heavy!" said Bailey. She could barely lift the first dusty carton. "What's in them?"

"Books," said Sugar. She took her glasses off and wiped them carefully on her red wool shirt.

"More books?" asked Bailey. Her grandmother's library was already filled to overflowing. There was no room on the shelves. Sugar's books were stacked on the floor and piled on tables. "Where are you going to keep them?" Bailey struggled to carry the first heavy box to the house.

"We'll pile as many as we can in the hall by the library—that's where I began stacking them this morning—then I guess we'll put some in the living room and others on the porch. I have one more batch to pick up," Sugar said.

"Another load?" Bailey wondered what her grandmother could be thinking. Even though they both liked to read, there was no way that they could finish all of them.

"What a deal I got!" said Sugar. She was out of breath from carrying the many cartons to the house. "The best bargain ever. After we bring in the rest, you and I'll go to Keswick Inn to have a talk with Will and Bekka. I have a terrific idea to discuss with them."

Bailey lugged the last carton to the hallway, and set it on top of the box she had tripped over earlier. She brushed dust off her yellow sweatshirt.

"I'll be ready in a few minutes," said Sugar.

"Okay," said Bailey. She decided to look for a bandage to put on her throbbing toe.

2

Perfect Mess

"Now are you going to tell me what's going on?" Bailey asked. Her toe still hurt, but not enough so that she couldn't walk with her grandmother through the woods to visit their neighbors, who owned Keswick Inn. Bailey's dog, Goldie, trotted behind them.

"I have a wonderful plan for all of us," said Sugar. "I'll explain it to everyone at the same time." She hummed a tune that Bailey didn't recognize.

Bailey couldn't imagine what Sugar's plan might be. Maybe Sugar wanted Will Keswick to enlarge her library for all the new books. Maybe her grandmother was planning to have a yard sale of her own and sell the books. Sugar continued humming and smiling. It was clear that Bailey would have to wait a few more minutes to find out. The path ended at the back of the orchard where tart apples were ready for harvest. Bailey could see the big and little barns and the country inn owned by Mr. Will and Miss Bekka, parents of her adopted, twelve-year-old friends, Noah and Fred, and their soon-to-be-adopted foster sister, Sparrow.

As they came closer she could see a goat, pig and rooster in their pens and the boys' little white dog, Clover, barking and racing to greet Goldie.

Mr. Will took off his blue cap and ran his fingers through his hair, the color of a yellow cat. "Hey, there," he said. "Come sit on the porch. Fred's brownies should be done in a minute."

"I'd rather we talk in the little barn, if you don't mind," said Sugar. "Where's everybody? I have something great to suggest."

Mr. Will look puzzled. "Sure. Bailey, please tell everyone to meet us there."

"Okay." Bailey ran to the house shouting for Noah, Fred, Miss Bekka and Sparrow. Bailey didn't wait for them to come out, but hurried back to the little barn with its unusual two-story roof.

Tall, thick weeds made it difficult for Mr. Will to open the creaky door all the way. He pushed and tugged until it groaned open and Bailey had her first look inside.

"We've been so busy fixing up the big barn for the animals and equipment storage that I haven't worked on this old building yet," he said.

Sugar peered over Bailey's shoulder. "Perfect," she announced.

"Perfect?" said Mr. Will. He turned to each wall, trying to see what Sugar saw. "Perfect? I'd say it's a mess. A big mess."

"It's just what we need," said Sugar.

"For what?" asked Bailey.

"For Sugar's Book Barn," announced her grandmother.

"Sugar's what?" asked Miss Bekka, walking through the doorway with Noah and Fred right behind her.

"I've been thinking," said Sugar. "Keswick Inn needs something special for its guests to enjoy while they're staying here. This little barn could be turned into a bookstore and gift shop. There's nothing like it within an hour's drive."

Bailey's hazel eyes widened. "So that's what all those book boxes are for," she said. "Now I get it!"

She pushed her medium-length brown hair behind her ears and looked around at her friends. The boys seemed equally astonished and pleased. "Great idea," said Fred. "I'll help."

"Me, too," said Noah, running his fingers through his yellowish hair that looked like Mr. Will's.

"Me, three," said Sparrow. Her wheelchair stopped just outside the doorway.

"Well, Will?" said Miss Bekka.

Mr. Will walked around the dark barn. A barn swallow swooped from the eves and nearly bumped into him. He touched the wall boards and studied the cobweb-draped rafters.

"It'll take quite a bit of work." He kicked at the broken strips of wood on the dirt floor.

Bailey watched Sugar's face. Her eyes were twinkling and she looked like she was saving her biggest smile for Mr. Will's answer.

"Of course I'll pay the costs," said Sugar.

Mr. Will walked over to a broken window and looked out. He ran his hands around the frame.

"I think we can fix it up without too much trouble. Justin will be available after school and on weekends, and the boys are good helpers. Sure," he said.

Sugar's face crinkled into a huge smile.

"Tell us about the books," said Miss Bekka. "I gather you already have some to sell?"

"Do I ever!" said Sugar. She leaned against the wall. "I saw an ad in the paper last week that a used-book store was closing up in Culpeper. The owner wanted to get rid of everything. So, while Bailey was in school, I took a ride, made an offer, and started hauling books home."

"What kind of books?" asked Fred.

"A little of this and a little of that. Most of them are used. Some may be rare. The owner wasn't really sure what he had anymore."

"Are there children's books for me?" asked Sparrow.

"A number of boxes of them," said Sugar. "And even though this is a store, you may come in and read anytime—free. We'll have a special reading corner for kids."

"There's got to be room for my wheelchair," said Sparrow.

"Indeed," said Sugar. "The store will be handicap accessible so everyone can come in."

"I want to help sell books," said Bailey.

"Of course," said her grandmother. "I was counting on that."

"I think this is a fantastic idea," said Miss Bekka. "We'll talk with local artists and they can sell their paintings, jewelry and pottery, if that's okay with you."

"That's the idea," said Sugar. "Something fun at the inn, and good for the community."

"We can start fixing it up in a week or so," said Mr. Will. "I'll see what needs to be done and I'll make a list of supplies."

"Fantastic!" said Sugar. "I've always wanted to run a bookstore. And now I will."

3

Work Begins

Within two weeks, Mr. Will, Noah, Fred and Justin, a neighborhood boy, had taken the trash that had been stored in the small barn to the landfill, and had installed insulation and new walls. The Keswicks hired experts to do the electrical wiring and roofing, but worked on the new wood floor themselves.

In the third week, Justin and Mr. Will made bookshelves for three walls, and bookcases to go in the center of the room.

The fourth wall, near the doorway, was where Sugar planned to put a table, her cash register on a small desk with drawers, a desk chair and two recliners. One recliner would be for Bailey, and the other would be a place for Sugar to sit and read when there were no customers in the shop.

Another table and shelves in the corner farthest from the door would display the special gifts for sale. Sugar left room on two walls for paintings by local artists.

She planned to put an assortment of her favorite new books on a table near the front so that she could recommend them to customers.

"Customers may also suggest books to me," she said. "We'll have great conversations, and perhaps we can start book discussion groups. Some for kids and some for adults."

"Count us in," said Miss Bekka.

Mr. Will also installed a small woodstove in one corner to heat the Book Barn during the winter.

Sugar bought red paint for the outside barn boards, and moss-green paint for the inside. The reading corner, however, would be painted orange and yellow. "Bright and cheerful," she said.

"I wish I could stay home and help you paint," said Bailey.

"There will be plenty to do after school and on weekends," said Sugar.

"Yes, but it isn't fair that Noah and Fred are homeschooled and can help work on the Book Barn when they're done with their classwork."

Sugar wrapped her arm around her. "They're busy studying most of the day, just like you. Now help me carry the paint cans inside."

~ ~ ~

Bailey rushed over every afternoon as soon as the school bus let her off at Sugar's driveway. She helped paint and tacked up posters that had pictures of books and encouraged reading.

Then one day, when Sugar was ready to bring boxes of books from her house to the shop, Mr. Will told Bailey that he had a surprise for her grandmother. Bailey made Sugar cover her eyes before they reached the little barn.

"You can look now!" said Bailey.

"Oh, my!" said her grandmother. "I can't believe it. Thank you, dear friends."

Above the door was a large shiny sign.

SUGAR'S BOOK BARN
MAKE YOURSELF COMFY AND READ

Another sign across the side of the barn read:

KESWICK INN GIFT SHOP

The signs were bright blue with black and gold letters. Sugar looked like she might cry.

"This is a dream come true," she said. "Now, Bailey and I have a lot of work to do to set up the store. Let's get going, girl."

"We'll help," offered Noah. The boys squeezed in the back seat of the cab of Sugar's pickup.

Bailey knew they must be as curious as she was about what kinds of books were in those bulging cardboard boxes.

4

Moving In

It took ten trips with the pickup to carry the rest of the boxes from Sugar's house to the Book Barn. Sugar said, "Enough for today. There're more cartons in my shed, but this will do for now."

Bailey could see that Fred and Noah looked relieved, even though they hadn't complained about the work.

"I'll start unpacking books tomorrow while Bailey's in school, and then you all can help me shelve them in the afternoon," Sugar said, wiping her brow with her sleeve.

She sat on one of the piles of boxes and looked around the room. "We need to decide on the types of sections and where they're going to go."

"We're good with books," said Fred.

"Not until I get here," said Bailey. "That's only fair."

"Why? Do you think we'll find a secret treasure and not tell you about it?" Noah grinned at her.

Bailey's face became hot. "No, it's just—" She looked at Sugar.

Sugar smiled warmly. "There's plenty of work for everyone before our grand opening in three weeks. Now, we're going to go back to the house to pick up the desk and chairs I stored in my shed."

"I wondered why you bought those at the yard sale," said Bailey.

"And you never asked," said Sugar. "You made it very easy for me to have my big surprise."

The two recliners, one dark green and the other beige, were awkward to lift, but not too heavy for Bailey, Fred and Noah to place in the back of the truck. On the second trip, Sugar helped them hoist the large wooden desk in the back along with four navy and yellow beanbag chairs that she said were for the children's section.

Sugar also tossed a large fuzzy tan pillow in the back. "This is for Goldie to sleep on when she visits the Book Barn," she said.

"She'll like that," said Bailey, rubbing her hound dog's ears.

"Now, my dear," said her grandmother, "it's time for you to do your homework and I need to fix supper.

"Can't we open just one box?" asked Fred.

"Tomorrow is soon enough," said Sugar. She turned off the light and closed the barn door.

5

E-mail from Mom

"I'm worn out," Sugar told Bailey when they got home. "Today I'm wondering if I'm getting too old for all this work."

Bailey was alarmed. "Do you feel okay? Do you want to sit down? Do you want me to call Miss Bekka?"

"Just kidding. Nothing that putting my feet up and reading a good book won't cure. Now that it's so much cooler at night, maybe this would be a good time to build a fire in the fireplace. What do you think?"

"That'd be great. I'll fix cocoa," said Bailey, somewhat relieved. A little piece of worry, however, settled in her heart.

"But first, supper," said Sugar. "Why don't you check your e-mail, and start your homework while I put something together."

Bailey quickly set the table before heading to Sugar's office to use the computer.

The only e-mail was from her mother, Molly, who was living and working in Costa Rica. Bailey sighed when she saw that her mother's note started with "Andrew," the name of the man she planned to marry.

From: Mollyf2@travl.net
To: "Bailey"<baileyfish@gmail.com>
Sent: 9:43 p.m.
Subject: galleys

Andrew and I are so excited about how well my book about him is coming. The publisher sent us galleys -- those are copies of the book before it is totally finished. The real cover isn't on it yet, and the galleys aren't for sale, but we get to see and hold them. Now my book seems much more real. Because I had two extra copies, I've sent them to you and Sugar. Aren't you proud of your mom? Hugs and kisses. Gotta go. Mom

Bailey sighed again. She *was* proud of her mom for getting a dream job and writing a book, even though it meant they were so far apart. Molly had left for Costa Rica quite suddenly in the winter, sending Bailey from Florida to Virginia to live with Sugar.

What Bailey didn't like was Dr. Andrew Snorge-Swinson, an entomologist. Bailey called him Bug Man. She wished her mother would break up with him so it would just be the two of them again when her mom returned for good.

"Supper's ready," called Sugar. "I heated up last night's leftover pasta with more homemade sauce."

Bailey logged off without answering her mother's message. She watched Sugar lift the noodles with her long tongs, and then ladle hot sauce over them in a green bowl.

Sugar's short hair was mussed up, as usual. Bailey looked at her grandmother's soft cheeks, pink from leaning over the pot of boiling water. She wanted to hug her grandmother, but she didn't want the tomato sauce to spill.

"Mom's sending us copies of a galley of her book," said Bailey, pulling out her chair.

"I had hoped she would," said her grandmother. "Because the galleys aren't the finished book, if we see any errors, we need to tell her so that the final edition will be perfect."

The only thing that would be perfect would be if Mom announced on the last page that she was done with Bug Man, thought Bailey.

6

Stranger in the Store

Noah, Fred and Sparrow were in Sugar's Book Barn when Bailey arrived. Sparrow was dusting children's books and talking with Sugar about where they should go. Noah and Fred were sorting books into piles they had labeled mystery, teen fiction, travel, cookbooks, nature, and novels.

"I want to read this one," said Fred. He studied the title of a green hardback book that was missing its jacket. *"The Ghost Light Flickered,"* he said. "The back cover says it's a theater mystery."

"Put it aside," said Sugar. "The pay isn't very good in my bookstore, but you can read all you want for free."

"I want these," said Sparrow. She had placed ten picture books in her pile.

"Sure, sweetheart," said Sugar.

"What do you want me to do?" asked Bailey.

She dropped her green book bag next to the bookshop door.

"You may help Fred and Noah. As soon as we get the books separated into categories, we'll organize them on the shelves in alphabetical order by author's last name," said Sugar.

"Just like a library," said Sparrow, adding two more books to the pile in her lap.

Bailey heard Goldie growl softly. She turned and looked at the doorway. Standing just inside was a tall woman with baggy pants and a green flannel overshirt with long sleeves. She had shoulder-length, dark frizzy hair and wore large sunglasses that covered half her face.

"Is the bookstore open for business?" she asked in a surprisingly deep voice.

"Not really," said Bailey.

"But welcome," called Sugar. "You are our first visitor. Feel free to come in and look around, but we're not open for business yet. The grand opening isn't for a few weeks."

"Thank you," said the woman, stepping inside.

"Is there anything in particular that you are looking for?" asked Sugar.

"I have my favorite authors," said the strange woman. "I'll just look around, if you don't mind."

Goldie had stopped growling, but the fur was still standing up on the back of her neck. Bailey pointed to her bed, and Goldie lay down, keeping her eyes on the visitor.

The woman quickly surveyed the piles of books that Noah and Fred were sorting, then asked Sugar, "Do you mind?"

"No, go ahead," said Sugar.

The woman opened one of the cartons, and examined its contents. Then she opened another and another. Bailey thought, *She'll be here all night. They're so many boxes.*

Finally the woman looked at her watch and said, "I'd best be going. I'll be back soon if that's all right."

"Join us for the grand opening on the seventh," Sugar said cheerfully.

The woman didn't answer. She was gone.

"She's strange," said Bailey.

"Well, you know what they say: Don't judge a book by its cover," said Sugar with a big smile. "And that applies to people, too."

"Okay, but Goldie didn't like her," said Bailey.

"Goldie's not used to having people come into the Book Barn just yet," said Sugar. "I don't expect her to like them all, but she'll need to learn to be polite." Sugar walked to the back of the store with a load of books with badly damaged covers.

"Hey, will you look at this!" exclaimed Noah.

He held up a hardcover book titled *Flight of the Turkey Wing,* by Oliver Cowrie.

"What about it?" asked Fred.

"It's hollow," said Noah. "It seems like a regular book with pages, but when you look inside, just past the first few pages, it's hollowed out, like something could be hidden."

"Let me look," said Bailey. He handed it to her. "I wonder what was in it?"

"Maybe jewels or gold," said Noah.

"Maybe they fell out and are in a box," said Bailey. "Let's see." She lifted out a few books, but saw nothing like it in the carton.

"No time to go through more books. Not today anyway," said Sugar, glancing at the clock.

"It's closing time. Now, Sparrow, show me what you're borrowing. Fifteen books? Do you think you'll be able to read them all tonight?"

"Yes," said Sparrow. "Miss Bekka and I like to read after supper."

"And if Mom's busy, Noah and I'll read with you," said Fred. "Sugar, do you mind if I buy *Flight of the Turkey Wing*?"

"Have at it," said Sugar. "Strange title, but books are often like that."

She turned out the light and locked the heavy wooden door.

7

Problems

Sugar's phone rang while Bailey was eating breakfast the next morning. "Oh, no!" Sugar said. "I'll be right over."

"What's the matter?" asked Bailey.

"It's probably nothing, but Will thinks someone was trying to get into the Book Barn."

"Why, what happened?" asked Bailey.

"It appeared that something was trying to cut the lock off. Will says Clover was scratching on the inn's door last night so he let her out, and then she barked and barked until he followed her to have a look."

"What are you going to do?" Bailey grabbed her books and lunch. The bus would be at the end of the driveway in just a moment.

"That's what we'll talk about when I get over there," said Sugar. "I just don't understand why anyone would want to break into a bookstore that isn't even open yet."

"Be careful," said Bailey. She kissed her grandmother and dashed out the door.

Her friend, Emily, had saved her a seat on the bus and Justin was sitting behind her, staring out the window. "You're all out of breath," said Emily. "I thought you were going to miss the bus."

"Sugar heard that someone tried to break into her bookstore last night," said Bailey, sliding into the seat.

Emily said, "That's terrible. Did they take anything?"

"I don't think so. There's not much to take, just old books," said Bailey. "Sugar says the brand-new books she's ordered will be here next week."

"That's so cool. I want to help out at the open house," said Emily. Before Bailey could say anything else, Emily quickly changed to a seat across the aisle so that she could talk with Marsha about basketball practice. The bus driver shook his finger at Emily, but didn't make her move back next to Bailey.

While she gazed out the window, Bailey wondered how long it would be before all the leaves came off the trees and it turned cold. It would still be hot then in Florida—maybe hot enough to go swimming with her best Florida friend,

Amber, if their mothers weren't too busy to take them to Englewood Beach. They enjoyed Saturday or Sunday all-day picnics together, spreading out their blankets as close to the water as they could get without letting the incoming tide wash over them. While their mothers lay on towels to talk, Bailey and Amber hunted for shark teeth and floated on foam noodles in the water.

Or maybe it isn't hot in Florida now. Bailey was having trouble remembering. It had been months since she had come to Virginia.

The bus pulled in at the end of a long line of yellow buses.

"See you in math," said Emily, grabbing her books and hurrying into the school with Marsha.

Bailey headed for her locker. She was still getting used to the combination. The first week of school she wrote it on the back of her wrist: L 8 R 3 L 6. The lock turned too easily and she often moved past her number and had to start over. "Rats!" she whispered, when it wouldn't open. "I'm going to be late." She rattled the handle and the door popped open.

Bailey stuffed her lunch bag inside. She looked at the new picture of her mother, with her thick, dark wavy hair, that she had taped inside the door. It was actually a picture of her mother and Bug Man, but Bailey had carefully cut him out of the photo. She could see part of his elbow, but that was all. Now she could pretend that her mother was smiling at just her, not at Bug Man, who was standing next to her with a large yellow butterfly on  his finger. His hand was out, like he was giving the butterfly to Molly as a special gift.

The bell rang. Bailey slammed the locker door and walked quickly to her first class.

8

Surprises

Sugar and Mr. Will were surveying the barn doorway when Bailey arrived after school. He had replaced the small lock with a large thick padlock and had hooked up a motion-detector light that would turn on if anything or anyone came near it.

"We'll be able to see who's near the barn from our house," he told Sugar. "And I'm also going to get a security alarm tomorrow, and a new door. No one will dare try to break in."

"I still don't know why someone would do it," said Sugar, "but I thank you for your help." She gave Bailey's shoulder a squeeze. "Wait till you see the progress I've made today."

Bailey stepped inside the doorway. She was astonished. Whole sections of shelves were neatly filled with books. There were still dozens of boxes that hadn't been opened yet. Sugar said that besides the brand-new books that were arriving soon, she had also purchased all the books that were being discarded by a city public library.

In the back of the first aisle labeled mysteries and travel, Noah and Fred were examining a book.

"Hey, Bailey, take a look at this. It's another one of those hollow books, and this one has a picture of a seashell in it and this little paper with letters on it," said Noah.

"What kind of shell?" asked Bailey.

"We've never seen one like it before," said Fred. "Here. See if you can figure it out." He pulled the papers from his pocket and handed them to Bailey.

Bailey studied the picture. The shell seemed to be about three inches high and it was shaped like an ice cream cone. It was white with rows of brown marks that looked like ancient hieroglyphics.

"That's an alphabet cone shell," said Bailey excitedly. "I saw them in the Shell Museum on Sanibel."

"An alphabet cone? I never heard of that," said Noah. He took the picture from her and looked at it more closely.

"I guess some of these shapes do look like letters," he said.

"Let me see," said his brother. "Wait! There *are* letters on it. "I see an M and that looks like a Y, and look, that could be an E."

"M Y E. E M Y. Y E M. What does it mean?" asked Noah. "And the paper has other letters."

"Let me see again," said Fred, pulling the paper from his hand.

"Careful," said Bailey. "Don't tear it. It's our only clue."

"Are you folks going to help me this afternoon, or just read?" called Sugar from the back of the shop.

"Coming," said Bailey. She whispered, "We should put this in a safe place. They might mean something."

"Here's the book it was in," Noah whispered back. "The author's name—Cowrie—is the same as the first book, but the title is different." He gave the book to Bailey.

"Hmm," she said. She studied the title: *The Haunted Spiny Jewelbox.*

"Very strange." She passed the book to Fred, who hurried to where Sugar was shelving books. "I found another book we'd like to buy," he said.

"It's yours," Sugar answered from the top of a stepladder. "Please hand me those wildlife books."

"Sure," said Bailey. The first three were part of a set of nature photography of the national parks. Next in the pile were books about identifying wildflowers and trees, a book about African animals, one about Costa Rican rain forests, and another about shells and fish in the Gulf of Mexico.

"There," said Sugar. "That looks better. Now for the horses."

Bailey looked around. "I don't see any books about horses."

"Perhaps you should look outside," said her grandmother.

Noah and Fred scrambled for the door with Bailey close behind.

A horse transport truck and trailer had pulled into the yard near the big barn and Mr.

Will was talking with the driver. The men walked to the back of the trailer and Mr. Will motioned to the boys and Bailey to come help. The horses stomped and whinnied when the driver went back inside. Sparrow wheeled her chair down the back porch ramp, spilling books from her lap. She hurried after them.

"Dad?" said Noah. He tugged on Mr. Will's windbreaker.

"Your mother and I thought it was time you learned to ride and these are rescue horses that need a good home," said Mr. Will. "We were able to get them for a good price, and several friends from Northern Virginia said they'd help pay for their expenses as long as they can come down to the lake and ride them."

"Cool," said Noah.

"I want to ride" said Sparrow. "What about me? I'm supposed to be in this stupid wheelchair for another year."

"You'll see," said Mr. Will.

Bailey heard the clanking of a metal gate within the trailer. She saw the driver snap a rope on a horse's halter. He walked the first horse down the ramp and handed the rope lead to Fred.

"This is Nelson," said Mr. Will, reading from a sheet of paper. Fred led the pinto to the grass.

"Nelson's so thin," said Fred. He let the horse drop his head to the lawn where the pinto found a few blades of tall grass to munch on.

Another gate squeaked open. The driver appeared and handed the lead of a light gray horse with black stockings and a black mane to Noah. Noah's green eyes sparkled with delight. He led the gray horse over to where Fred was stroking his black-and-white spotted animal.

"Let's see, this one is Traveller," Mr. Will read from the paper.

"Traveller. Hmm, that name's familiar," said Noah.

"Do a little research, Son," said Mr. Will.

"Research?" asked Noah, stroking Traveller's mane.

"That's right," said his dad. "Do your home-work."

Bailey leaned against the fence and watched the boys with their horses. The "twins," as they liked to call themselves, seemed to have forgotten about her as they rubbed the horses. They didn't look entirely happy as they studied the condition of the animals. Fred's brown face showed worry. Noah's fair skin had flushed with the chilly air and he frowned.

"They're so thin," Noah said. "Look at those ribs showing."

"Don't worry. In addition to hay, we'll give them special food, such as sweet feed—grain mixed with molasses—to help them fill out," said Mr. Will.

Bailey had only been on top of a horse once and that was at a fireman's carnival. A woman with a long blond ponytail had walked Bailey's horse around a small ring twice, very slowly, while Bailey's mom took pictures and waved. Now she wondered if the boys would let her ride their horses, or if she and Sparrow would just have to watch.

Mr. Will went inside the horse trailer and another gate clanked. He poked his head out and said, "Here's something special for Sparrow. Do you think you can handle Meatball?"

The driver led a short gray pony with a very shaggy mane down the steps and handed the lead to Sparrow. "For me? It's really for me?" asked the seven-year-old. "A forever pony?" She sounded like she was going to cry. She brushed her long hair out of her face.

"He's yours to ride until you're too big to sit on him," said Mr. Will.

Bailey smiled at the little girl's happiness, but in her heart she felt a twinge of jealousy. She really wanted a horse of her own, but she wasn't one of the Keswicks—just a next-door neighbor. Bailey felt Sugar's comforting hands on her shoulders.

Just then, Mr. Will said, "Bailey, don't look so disappointed. Come over here."

Bailey walked quickly to the trailer. "Close your eyes, and hold out your hand," said Mr. Will. Bailey heard clomping down the ramp.

"Polly Peachum needs a special person—you," said Mr. Will.

Bailey felt a rope in her palm. She opened her eyes and looked into the large dark eyes of a brown horse with a white blaze on her face. The horse's head drooped as if she were too tired or weak to stand any longer. Bailey put her cheek next to the long face. "I'll take care of you, Polly Peachum," she whispered. Her heart glowed with happiness.

9

Getting Acquainted

"Why the sad look?" asked Miss Bekka. She placed a bucket of carrots and apples cut into pieces near the fenced-in area connected to the barn.

"It's just that the horses look so hungry and tired," said Bailey.

"We'll nurse them back to health," said Miss Bekka. "You'll all help with that. And, although each of you is responsible for one, the horses will eventually be for the guests of Keswick Inn to ride, also. Understand?"

"Sure, Mom," said Fred. "This is awesome." He stood on the bottom rail and reached out his palm with an apple in it. "Here, Nelson," he called out. The pinto shook his head and plodded to the fence. He carefully removed the apple from Fred's hand and snorted. Juice dribbled from the corners of his mouth and he nudged Fred for another apple.

"Three more are due tomorrow—Old Baldy, Little Sorrell, and Liberty—and after that, Vic and Dandy, " said Mr. Will. That way all of us can ride together, including Sugar and Justin."

"Great names," said Sugar, giving Will a knowing smile. The smile made Bailey curious about what the names meant.

Sugar leaned on the fence. "It's been a long time since I've been on a horse," she said, "but I'm willing to try. I'll need a mounting block to get on. I don't think I can reach the saddle without steps."

"What's the story about the horses, Dad?" asked Noah.

"They were removed from a farm where a lot of animals—cats, dogs, goats, cows, but not Meatball—were found starving. The veterinarian feels that these horses will be totally okay in a few months. In the meantime, we'll give them lots of tender loving care."

"Do we have to keep the names?" asked Sparrow. She had tied Meatball's rope to her wheelchair and led the pony near Miss Bekka's bucket so she could fish out the biggest carrot for him.

"You can name them whatever you like," said Miss Bekka, "or call them by the names they came with."

"I'm not sure about the name Meatball. I like Muffin, or maybe Sparky. I don't know. This is hard," said Sparrow.

"Take your time. It doesn't have to be today," said Fred, tugging gently on her sweatshirt hood.

"He doesn't look like a meatball. I'll just call him Pony for now," said Sparrow.

10

Daydreaming

Bailey had to bang her locker twice to get it to pop open the next morning. "Rats!" she whispered. "I don't want to be late for math."

Although she really liked her teacher and had no difficulty working the problems, she hadn't focused very well when she studied for the quiz. First she thought about her sad horse, then about the shell picture in the hollowed-out book that Fred said was called a book safe. She couldn't wait for school to be over so she could get back to the big barn to check on the horses and other animals, and to see what was going on in Sugar's Book Barn.

Mr. Renick passed out the test questions. Bailey quickly got to work, forcing herself to concentrate.

"Time's up. Pass your paper to the person on the left for scoring. Then I'll read the answers," Mr. Renick said.

Bailey was relieved that she only missed one. Her mind drifted back to the alphabet cone.

What did the museum tour guide tell us about that shell? Oh, some also have numbers. Some alphabet cones seem to spell out words because they may have more than one letter on them.

Bailey thought about walking on the Gulf beach at sunrise with her mother. They never found an alphabet cone shell, but many mornings they filled their pockets with surprises that had washed in with the tide: limpets, lightning whelks, goldies, worm snails, tulips, conchs and scallops. They threw shells with live creatures inside back into the water. They later sprayed the nonliving shells with a hose and set them in the sun to dry.

"Aren't they wonderful treasures?" Molly would say. "Mother Nature is so good to us."

At home Bailey placed her favorite ones on a bookshelf and stored others in a shoe box in her closet.

Mr. Renick cleared his throat. Bailey realized he was standing next to her desk. "Bailey, you seem to be a thousand miles away. Please return to Louisa, Virginia. We'd like the pleasure of your company."

Bailey's face reddened when she heard laughter.

"Sorry, Mr. Renick," she said.

He smiled kindly and walked back to the whiteboard. "Not much homework this weekend," he said. "The weather is too beautiful. Go outside and enjoy—after you work the problems on page 84."

Bailey quickly jotted the page number in her assignment book. *It will be great to be outside with the new horses. I wonder how Polly Peachum is feeling? She looked so bad yesterday,* Bailey thought. She jumped up when the bell rang.

11

Molly's Book

Sugar had left a note for Bailey telling her that she would be unpacking more books and to join her and Goldie at the shop.

Bailey quickly changed into old jeans and her green sweatshirt She grabbed two peanut butter cookies from a Santa cookie jar that Sugar had just bought for a dollar at a yard sale. She dashed out the door and jogged along the path between Sugar's house and Keswick Inn. Golden, brown and red leaves crunched beneath her feet. They were continuing to cover the lawn. Sugar had told her at breakfast that morning that they would need to rake the yard at least one more time before winter.

Bailey could see the three horses and the pony grazing in the pasture beyond the big barn. Sparrow was watching them through the fence boards, and Noah and Fred were leaning on the top rail.

"How're they doing?" asked Bailey. She was breathing hard from the run.

"Difficult to tell," said Noah. "They don't seem as nervous as they did yesterday—like they're beginning to feel safe here."

"I've changed my pony's name," said Sparrow, tugging on Bailey's sleeve.

"Three times already," said Fred with a big grin.

"His new name is Snorkel," Sparrow said.

"Why?" asked Bailey.

"Just because," said Sparrow. "I think it's funny."

"Me, too," said Fred, rumpling Sparrow's dark-blond hair.

"Polly Peachum still doesn't look very well," said Bailey. "She hangs her head like she isn't strong enough to lift it up."

"I'm sure she'll be okay. Dad said he'll call the large-animal veterinarian again if he needs to," Noah said.

Bailey nodded, but she still felt worried. *What if something happens to Polly?*

"The other rescued horses are coming later this afternoon," said Fred. "I guess we'd better help your grandmother until then."

Bailey gave the horses another long look before following the boys to the Book Barn.

"I'm glad you're here," Sugar said. "I need help hanging artwork. And Bailey, have a look at what's in the package on the front desk." She motioned to the boys to pick up oil paintings that were leaning against her recliner.

Bailey saw the padded envelope with Costa Rican stamps had already been opened. She reached inside and pulled out a book. It was the bound galley that her mom had promised.

On the cover was a picture of Bug Man, with his thick glasses and ponytail, and there were also three smaller pictures of insects and butterflies. Bug Man was holding a magnifying glass. Bailey frowned when she read the title in bold letters: *Living with the Leaf Cutters: The*

Amazing Life of Dr. Andrew Snorge-Swinson. At the bottom of the cover was her mother's name: Molly T. Fish.

Printed information on the back cover said that these were uncorrected page proofs and that the book would be available next year and that there would be tours and interviews.

Bailey looked inside. On the very first page, her mother had handwritten in bright green ink: *For my darling Bailey, who has always been there for me, even when I haven't been there for her. I hope you're proud, and I know you'll love Andrew. Mom*

Bailey was proud, but why did her mom always have to bring Andrew into everything?

"Well, what do you think?" asked Sugar, giving her a special grandmother hug. "She autographed a copy to me, too."

"It's okay," said Bailey, turning the pages. The center section had color pictures of Costa Rican insects and views of the rain forest. There were pictures of Bug Man at work observing leaf cutter ants, and pointing out giant termite nests.

Bailey flipped to the back. There was a page about the author, Molly, with a beautiful picture of her sitting outside with a butterfly on her shoulder.

The words talked about all of Molly's experiences as a writer, and mentioned that she had a daughter.

They could have said what her daughter's name is, thought Bailey. Hot tears blurred her eyes. *They didn't even print my name in her book.*

"Let me see," said Noah. Bailey handed him her copy. "This is so great. Your mom—a writer. Maybe Sugar will sell it in the store."

"Great idea," said Sugar. "I'm sure we can work it out after the book is published."

"I can't wait to read it," said Fred.

"Here," said Bailey. She handed him her copy.

"Don't you want to look at it first?" he asked. Sugar's eyebrows raised in surprise and she looked at Bailey.

"I've got other things to read right now, like *Misty of Chincoteague*, and—"

"Bailey and I can share my copy," said Sugar.

Bailey walked over to an unopened carton of books.

"Go ahead and sort that box, Bailey," said Sugar. "I have no idea what's in it. I'll be back there to help in a few minutes."

12

The Stranger Returns

"Look, here's another of those weird books," Bailey said. "You know, the book safes." As Fred and Noah rushed back to have a look, Bailey opened it and saw creased picture of an alphabet cone shell.

"It's not the same shell," said Bailey. "Look, it has the letters M A E."

"The author is the same—Oliver Cowrie—but this book is called *The Last of the Junonia Dreams,*" whispered Noah. "We'd better hide it until we can figure this all out."

"I took the first two to my room," Fred said softly. "Did anyone look in the box to see if another picture might have fallen out?"

"I think that carton is still out in the trash pile. I'll check it in a minute," said Bailey.

The bells jingled at the door announcing a visitor to the bookshop. Sparrow entered, followed by the tall woman.

"That lady is back and she wants to know if the bookstore is open now," said Sparrow, wheeling inside. "I told her it was okay to come in."

"We're truly not quite ready for customers," said Sugar, walking to the woman. "Do you mind coming back another time?"

"I just want to look through a few more boxes while I'm in the area," said the woman in a voice as rough as sandpaper.

"I'd like to help you but we're really in the middle of things right now," Sugar replied. "If you could tell me what books or authors you're searching for, I'd be glad to give you a call if something turns up."

The woman thought for a moment, then said, "Cowrie is one of my favorites." The woman took a pen out of her bag and wrote down her phone number. "Please do call if you locate any of his works."

"Will do, and be sure to return for the grand opening," said Sugar.

The bells jingled and the woman was gone with a slight wave of her hand.

"Cowrie?" whispered Bailey to the twins. "That's the author's name on the hollow books."

"Yes," Fred replied quietly. "We'd better buy all of them before someone else does." He put

The Last of the Junonia Dreams behind his back and tucked it under his shirt.

"I've got money for this one," said Noah.

"I'll pay for the next one if we find more," said Bailey.

"Good idea," said Noah.

"Sugar, what did you say the hardback books cost?" asked Fred.

"Oh, two dollars each, unless they are brand new," she replied.

Fred rummaged in his pockets. "I've three dollars right now and I'll give you the rest tomorrow," he said.

"Your credit is good," said Sugar. "I hear a truck. I'll bet it's the other horses. Let's go have a look. But do you mind unpacking the rest of that box first, Fred?"

"Sure, Sugar," he said, handing her his money.

He whispered to Noah and Bailey, "Meet you at the pasture after I help Sugar. Would you take this to my room, bro? We can look at them later."

Noah nodded and concealed the book under his arm.

"See ya after I look for that box in the trash pile," said Bailey.

13

Time with Polly

The new horses, a dapple gray, a palomino, and a jet-black stallion, were also thin and tired.

Mr. Will checked their mouths and hooves after they came out of the transport van. "Liberty needs better shoes, and Old Baldy's missing teeth," he said. "I think they'll be fine with proper care and the right food."

"Polly Peachum still looks kinda sick," said Bailey. Mr. Will turned and studied the horses grazing in the pasture. Bailey pointed and he saw the droopy head.

"Why don't you take Polly a pan of alfalfa pellets and pet her for a while. I think she needs some special attention," he said. "And tomorrow Miss Bekka will show you how to groom her with the currycomb. It will help clean her coat."

Bailey smiled with surprise. She found the feed sack and a bumpy old pan next to it. After filling it with feed pellets, she opened the gate to the pasture and walked slowly over to Polly. The horse didn't move away. Flies swarmed around her head.

Bailey said softly, "It's okay, girl. I'm Bailey, and I've brought you treats." She held out the pan. Polly Peachum sniffed, then put her nose in the pan, dropping a few on the muddy ground. Bailey smiled as the rest of the food disappeared. The horse then jerked her head and stepped backwards.

Bailey felt something brush her leg and looked down. "What are you doing here? Did you slip under the fence?" she asked Goldie. The dog wagged her tail. "Okay, you can stay with me but don't scare the horses."

Goldie whined and sat at Bailey's feet. Bailey placed the empty pan next to the hound, and reached her hand out to the mare. Polly Peachum didn't move so Bailey walked closer until she could rub her velvety nose.

"I'm your friend. And when you are strong, I'm going to ride you, even though I don't know much about riding." Polly Peachum's eyes closed. Bailey stroked her neck and looked at her bony sides.

"You're doing a fine job," said Miss Bekka. "That's what Polly girl needs right now."

Bailey said, "I didn't hear you come up, Miss Bekka."

"I didn't mean to surprise you," the boys' mother said.

"Did you ride a lot when you were my age?" asked Bailey.

"At eleven, quite a bit. I had my own horse, but it was boarded in the country. I always dreamed of owning a stable and having my own horses, and now my dream is coming true." She rubbed Polly Peachum's neck. The horse flicked her ears.

"I guess your guests will like riding them," said Bailey. She wished Polly belonged to her, and just her alone.

"As time goes on, we'll have lots of things for families to do here," said Miss Bekka. "The lake, boating, horseback riding, the goat, pig, rooster, and hens on the way so that we can offer fresh eggs for breakfast."

"And don't forget the Book Barn," said Bailey.

"Especially, the Book Barn. Our guests will really enjoy that," said Miss Bekka. "By the way, I'd like you to help me think of a special surprise for your grandmother at the opening."

"Like what?" asked Bailey. She pulled an apple out of her pocket and offered it to Polly.

The horse's lips curled back and she carefully took the apple from Bailey's flat palm.

"That's why I need help. I can't think of anything really fun. Give it some thought." Miss Bekka handed Bailey a carrot, and walked back toward the big barn.

14

More Clues

"Did you find anything?" Noah asked Bailey while they waited for Fred near the pasture.

"Just this," she said. "I think it was in the carton that had the first book in it." She handed Noah a scrap of yellowed paper.

"I don't see anything on it," he said, "but it's the same kind of paper."

"Look again," Bailey said. "It doesn't have a picture of an alphabet cone shell, but there are letters on it."

Noah held the paper up to the light. "It looks like someone has written O, G and T. This is really strange."

"I know. Maybe we need to put all the letters together to see if they spell something," suggested Bailey.

"Great idea," said Noah, looking back at the barn. "Here comes Fred. You've got to get more exercise, bro. You're huffing."

Fred said, "You'd be out of breath if you'd been running, too. Look what I found." He held out his hand.

"Wow!" said Bailey.

"Let me see it," said Noah.

Fred handed him an alphabet cone shell.

"Where did you find it?" asked Noah. He handed the shell to Bailey, who squinted as she held it up to study the letters.

"I found one more of those book safes," said Fred. "It thumped when I took it out of the carton. When I opened it, there was the shell inside. And get this, the title of the book is *Angel Wings at Dawn* by Cowrie. Another strange title by the same author dude."

"This is so cool," said Bailey, rubbing the alphabet cone. "It's just like the ones I saw in the Shell Museum. I see a Y, and an E on it."

"Look again," said Fred. "I also saw an X. And that's not all I found." He reached in his pocket and pulled out an even larger shell that also had strange markings on it.

"What's this?" asked Noah.

"I'm not sure," said Fred. "It looks like it has exclamation points and commas, and maybe smiley faces."

"A punctuation shell?" asked Noah, grinning.

"No such thing," said Bailey, "but the mark-ings might be part of the clues to what the alphabet cone is trying to explain." She studied the second shell. "Maybe we should tell Sugar. She might have some ideas."

"Not just yet," said Noah. "Let's see what we can figure out first, then we'll show her. We're the detectives, remember?"

"We need to spread out all the clues—all the letters," said Fred.

"Speaking of clues, I know about Traveller," said Bailey. "I did research just like your father said."

"What about Traveller?" asked Noah. The smile left his face.

"Traveller was the name of a horse that belonged to General Robert E. Lee," said Bailey.

"I knew I should know that name," said Noah. He sounded annoyed that Bailey had learned something about his horse first.

"And, I know something else," said Bailey. "I looked up Polly Peachum."

"Who owned her? The queen of England?" asked Fred.

"Nope, that was the name of one of President Thomas Jefferson's riding horses. He had a whole bunch of them."

"What about the others?" asked Noah.

"Aren't you supposed to be looking them up for homeschool? I haven't had time to find out yet," said Bailey, "but I think the horses all have famous names."

"Except whatever Sparrow calls her pony," said Fred. "He's 'Sneakers' today because he's smelly."

"Now, let's write down all the letters and see what we can figure out," said Bailey. "I've got to get home before dark."

15

Worries

Bailey returned from Keswick Inn, stomped the mud off her shoes and left them on the back porch. Sugar covered her chicken casserole with foil and placed it in the oven.

"There. It'll be ready in about an hour. I think I'll take a little nap before dinner," Sugar said. "Don't let me oversleep."

"Okay," said Bailey. She'd have time to finish her math problems before supper.

Goldie padded up the stairs after Bailey and hopped on the bed. Bailey took the crumpled paper from her pocket and smoothed it out. She had jotted down the alphabet cone letters when she and the twins hadn't been able to come up with anything that made sense when they met briefly at the pasture. After studying the letters again for a few seconds, she slid the paper under her dictionary while she worked on her homework.

If only her mother were here. Molly was so good at word games and puzzles. She would figure out the mystery in a few tries. Bailey opened her math book.

She looked out the window. Long shadows fingered the yard. She wondered if Sugar was feeling okay. She rarely napped in the afternoon, even when she seemed tired.

Shadow jumped up on the desk and swatted at Bailey's pencil with his gray paw.

"You'll make me mess up my problems, you silly cat," said Bailey. Shadow played with the pencil until it fell on the floor and his sister, Sallie, pounced on it. "Good thing I have more," said Bailey. "Now leave me alone until I'm done, then we'll play the yarn game."

Bailey worked the problems. "They're easy," she told her cats.

The phone rang. Bailey continued with the homework, expecting her grandmother to answer it. But the phone rang and rang and then Bailey could hear someone leaving a message on the answering machine.

Where's Sugar? Why hasn't she answered the phone? Bailey was suddenly worried. She hurried down the stairs and into Sugar's library. Sugar was sleeping soundly in her recliner. Her glasses had fallen on the floor.

"Sugar, are you all right?" Bailey touched her grandmother's shoulder.

Sugar jumped. "What's happening?"

"Didn't you hear the phone?" asked Bailey. She bent down to give Sugar a kiss on the cheek. "Your face is really hot," Bailey said. "Are you sick?"

"I feel a little achy. Maybe I'm coming down with a cold or something," said Sugar.

Bailey handed her her glasses.

"Oh, my, just look at the time. Supper must be done," said Sugar, glancing at her watch. She stood up, and grabbed the back of the chair.

"Sugar, what's the matter?"

"I'll be okay. Just a little woozy. Probably got up too quickly. Now, please turn off the oven. Get the big mitts and carefully take out the casserole. Don't burn yourself. I'll be right along."

Bailey gave her grandmother a worried look and went into the kitchen. She carefully placed the steaming dish on a hot mat on the table and found a serving spoon in a drawer.

Sugar slowly made her way into the room and steadied herself with a chair before sitting down.

Bailey served both of them chicken legs and rice covered with homemade tomato sauce. She worried even more when Sugar ate only half of her meal and said she was going back to her recliner to rest.

"Shouldn't we call a doctor?" asked Bailey, "or Miss Bekka?"

"Let's see how I feel in the morning. Sorry to be such a party pooper. I have so much work to do tonight."

"I'll help you," offered Bailey.

"You're a dear," said Sugar. "I'll be okay. Just take care of the dishes and we'll see about things tomorrow."

16

Bus Ride

Sugar did seem better in the morning. She was humming in the kitchen when Bailey, followed by Shadow and Sallie, came downstairs for breakfast. Goldie was already in the kitchen, waiting patiently by her dish.

"See, I'm fine," said Sugar. She stirred oatmeal one more time before dishing it into two bowls.

Bailey kissed her cheek. "You still feel hot," she said.

"Must be from standing over the stove," said her grandmother. "Now hurry up or you'll be late for the bus."

"Are you sure you don't want me to stay home with you?" asked Bailey. She quickly swallowed her cereal.

"Not to worry," said Sugar.

Bailey grabbed her heavy gray zippered jacket and her book bag and hurried for the door just as the bus stopped at the end of the drive-way. *I wish today were a Saturday so I could stay home and make sure that Sugar's okay.*

Emily had saved a seat for her. Bailey slid in and zipped her sweatshirt.

"When can I ride your horse?" asked Emily. She pushed her dark curly hair out of her face and tucked it behind her ears with an orange headband.

"None of us can ride them yet," said Bailey. "Except Sparrow. Her pony's strong enough but ours are still getting well."

"When's that going to be?" Emily asked.

"I really don't know. Soon I hope. My horse, Polly Peachum, is pretty droopy."

"Polly Peachum—a dumb name," muttered Gabe, who was sitting next to Justin. He snickered, then said, "Ow! Stop poking me."

Bailey smiled and looked past Emily out the window. She figured Justin, who had a way with animals, was sticking up for the horses and their names, as odd as they were. She planned to learn more about the rest of the names soon, but Noah and Fred were only trying to figure out words that might be made from the alphabet cones' letters.

"What happens to your horse when you go back to live with your mom?" asked Emily.

Bailey jerked around to look at her. It wasn't anything she wanted to talk about with Emily or anyone, even though Emily sounded genuinely concerned. Fortunately, the bus door opened and Emily changed seats to be near Marsha, leaving Bailey by herself. She slid over to the window and pressed her nose against the already-smudged glass.

What would happen to Goldie, Sallie and Shadow and now Polly? What would happen to Sugar if she left? When she had moved to Virginia in the winter, what she wanted most was to return to Florida and be with her mother. But everything was so complicated now. Her mother was engaged to awful Bug Man who was allergic to animals. Bailey had new friends and her very own pets. They needed her and so did Sugar. What would happen to everyone without her?

"Bailey, you're going to be late," said Mr. Webster, the bus driver.

Bailey had been so deep in thought that she hadn't realized that the bus had stopped at the school. It was empty and her friends had run on ahead without her.

"Oops," she said, smiling at him. She dashed to the front door of the school and down the hall to her locker.

"Rats!" she said, when it wouldn't budge. She banged on it, and it popped open. Her mother's picture fell to the floor. Bailey's eyes stung when she picked it up and tossed it back inside.

17

Alone in the Store

Sugar was resting in her library when Bailey came home from school.

"Did you call the doctor?" asked Bailey.

"I did. He said it sounded like a bad cold or maybe the flu. I should feel better in a couple of days." Sugar coughed harder than she had in the morning.

"I'll fix supper," said Bailey.

"That would be great," said Sugar, "but first, do you mind opening the Book Barn? I'm expecting another big delivery. Miss Bekka or the boys can help you out if you need them. Take my cell phone so you can call me."

"Sure," said Bailey. She was pleased that Sugar trusted her to help out in the store.

Bailey took three peanut butter cookies out of the cookie jar and called to Goldie.

The air had a chill to it. It made her forehead feel funny for a moment, like when she licked a cone of key lime frozen yogurt at her favorite ice cream store on Sanibel.

Goldie stayed close to her as they ran through the woods to the Keswicks'.

Sugar had told her where the spare key to the Book Barn was hidden. It didn't take Bailey long to find it and open up the store. *Wish my locker opened that easily,* she thought.

The little barn seemed dark and cold without Sugar inside waiting for her. Bailey flicked on the lights. She rubbed her hands together. Then she remembered to turn on the red neon OPEN sign so the deliveryman would know someone was there, and she raised the shades on the front windows.

The floor creaked when she walked to Sugar's desk and the cash register.

I guess I could read a book while I'm waiting. Or maybe I should put more books away. There are still a few boxes left in the back.

Goldie sniffed the thick braided rug Sugar had placed near the door for people to dry their feet. Then she walked over to her bed, sighed and settled down where she could watch Bailey.

The clock showed it was four. When the store opened, the hours would be from three to five Wednesday through Friday, ten to two on Saturday, and a few Sunday afternoons.

Maybe I should call the Keswicks. No, Sugar thinks I'm old enough to take care of the Book Barn by myself. Goldie's here to protect me. I'll be fine.

But Bailey didn't feel fine. The Book Barn seemed much larger and quieter than she had expected.

She decided to read near the front door, rather than go into the back of the store by herself.

Sugar had placed several favorites on a table near the cash register. Most were adult fiction, but she also had a pile for kids. They featured horse stories: *Black Beauty; Black Gold; Horse on the Hill; Misty of Chincoteague;* and *Horses Horses Horses.*

Bailey smiled. Sugar must know that all the kids would be excited about the new horses and would want to read horse stories. She must have set these books aside when she was going through the boxes. Sugar had even written notes as bookmarks in each one, explaining why she liked the book so much.

Bailey opened *Horse on the Hill.* Sugar's note said it was out of print and hard to locate, but she thought Bailey would like it because the main character, Midge, was staying with her grandparents for the summer. Bailey decided to start with that one. She settled down in Sugar's recliner and leaned back. Just as she was reading about Midge spotting the mysterious horse on the hill, a sudden cold draft filled the Book Barn when the door was flung open.

Bailey jumped and squinted. She had trouble identifying the tall dark figure in the doorway because of the bright outside light.

"May I help you?" Bailey asked politely.

"I'm looking for the owner," said a deep voice, as the figure stepped inside onto the braided rug. Bailey froze with recognition. Goldie bounded to her and growled quietly.

"She'll be back in a minute," said Bailey, not wanting to admit she was alone.

"I'll wait," said the woman. "I believe she may have something I need."

"Actually, it might be more than a minute," said Bailey. "Why don't you come back tomorrow."

"I'll just wait, if you don't mind."

"Sure. Would you like to sit down and read a magazine or something?"

The woman didn't answer, but stood next to the door.

Bailey's fingers found Goldie's collar. "Hush," she whispered to her softly growling dog.

"The store really isn't ready yet," Bailey said. "I think my grandmother told you about the grand opening soon. It's going to be really great."

The woman didn't say anything. She tapped her fingers on her leg.

"We're going to have refreshments and entertainment, and maybe famous authors," Bailey continued, wishing someone—anyone— would come in or call. She glanced at the clock. *When would that delivery guy show up?* Goldie's growls rumbled from within. *Maybe she shouldn't have told the white lie that Sugar was coming right back. But what should she have said?* Bailey's voice was creeping down her throat where it couldn't be found. She wanted it to say, "Please go away, you frighten me," but it wouldn't.

The woman looked at her watch and toward the back of the store, then at the clock. She turned and glanced out the window near the door.

"Famous authors?" the woman finally asked in a husky voice. "Who?"

Bailey tried to think of some but her mind went blank. Then her voice came back and she blurted out, "Molly Fish. She's going to do her first booksigning here."

"Molly Fish? I never heard of her."

"That's because her book isn't out yet. Her book's about the famous Dr. Andrew Snorge-Swinson and his bugs, I mean, his study of insects," said Bailey.

Just then she heard the sound of a vehicle in the driveway and talking and laughter. It was the twins and Miss Bekka. They were headed for the Book Barn.

"I guess I'd better be going," said the woman with the deep voice. "I'll return for the grand opening, and to meet this famous author of yours." With that, she pulled the door open and left.

"Hey," said Noah, a moment later. "Wasn't that the woman who was looking for books by that author—Oliver Cowrie? What's she doing back here?"

Bailey shrugged.

"And where's Sugar?" asked Fred.

"Is everything all right, Bailey?" asked Miss Bekka.

Bailey nodded, then said, "Sort of."

18

Bailey's Idea

Bailey told them about Sugar not feeling well, and the strange woman, leaving out the part about how she had been afraid of her and of being in the Book Barn by herself. Then she asked, "Miss Bekka, remember when you said we should do something special for Sugar for her grand opening—that I needed to think of an idea? Well, what if we ask my mom to come for a booksigning as a big surprise for Sugar?"

Miss Bekka was quiet for a minute, then said, "Bailey, I think that's fantastic. Let me work on it, but don't tell anyone else or they might spoil the surprise. I'm sure if there is any possible way for your mom to be here, she'll do it for Sugar."

Bailey nodded.

"Now, I'll help you close up, and give you a ride home," said Miss Bekka. "That will let me check on Sugar myself."

"But what about the delivery of the books?" asked Bailey.

"Oh, they came early—right after lunch," said Miss Bekka. "Will and Noah put them in the back of the store on top of all the other boxes. I'm sorry. I thought Sugar knew."

"What about feeding Polly Peachum?" asked Bailey. "I was supposed to help out with her this afternoon."

"I'll do it," said Fred.

"I'll groom her," said Noah.

"You're the best," said Bailey. She waved and climbed in the van with Miss Bekka. Goldie sat at her feet and put her head in Bailey's lap.

"I'll need your mom's e-mail address and a phone number for her if you can get it. I know communication can be difficult where she's staying," said Miss Bekka. She turned the van around and headed out the driveway.

"I hope Mom isn't too busy to come," said Bailey.

"It is short notice, but you never know what might happen when you have a good idea," said Miss Bekka. "I was glancing at your copy of her galley that you loaned to Fred. It really is very well written." She seemed to be waiting for Bailey to say something about the book, but Bailey sank into the seat and looked out the window. *What if Mom doesn't want to come? But what if she does come? She'll want to show off her ring and talk about the wedding. It won't be a fun surprise for Sugar if Mom only talks about her plans.*

Miss Bekka parked next to Sugar's house. "Let's go see how your grandmother's feeling," she said. "And try to get that information for me while I'm talking with her." She put her arm around Bailey's shoulders as they walked up the steps.

19

Checking on Sugar

"Is it suppertime already?" Sugar reached for her glasses and peered at the mantel clock. "I guess I've been asleep all afternoon." She coughed deeply.

Bailey leaned down to give her a kiss. "You don't feel as hot," she said.

"Told you I'd feel better," said Sugar sitting up straighter. "You could fix me a cup of tea, though, and one for Bekka."

Bailey gave Miss Bekka a quick smile and went to the kitchen, leaving the two women to talk.

While the mugs of water were heating in the microwave, she looked in Sugar's address book near the kitchen phone. She found the cell phone listed for Molly Fish, and copied the number on a piece of scrap paper. Then she carefully printed her mother's e-mail address, which she knew by heart, and folded the paper. She returned to the library with the tea.

When Sugar was dunking her tea bag in hot water, Bailey slipped the paper to Miss Bekka. Her look said, "Nice work."

Bailey pulled up a chair.

Sugar took a deep sip. "How did things go in the shop this afternoon?" she asked Bailey. "I so appreciate your help today."

Bailey wondered if she should tell everything, or would news of the strange woman's arrival worry Sugar? Because Miss Bekka was listening, Bailey decided that she'd better tell her grandmother what happened.

"It was fine. I didn't know it but the shipment of books was already there. So, I started reading one of the horse books by the cash register when that tall woman came back. She said you had something she wanted," Bailey said.

Sugar took a long sip. "Really! She's an odd one. I've told her several times that we won't be ready for customers until the day of the open house."

"That's what I told her, too," said Bailey. She almost blurted out, "Because there will be a famous author here," but stopped herself in time.

"Bailey handled things well," said Miss Bekka with a big smile. "You can be very proud of her. Now, may I help with supper before I head back home?"

"Bailey and I can manage, thanks," said Sugar. "She's my wonderful all-around helper."

"Do I get a raise?" asked Bailey with a grin.

"When I make my first million in the Book Barn," said Sugar, coughing.

20

Planning the Surprise

Polly Peachum lifted her head when Bailey called to her from the fence. Now that Sugar was feeling better and back in the Book Barn, Bailey knew it was all right to spend time with her horse after school. Bailey called Polly again and held out a carrot. Polly's ears flicked and she snorted.

"C'mon, Polly. Good girl. I've got something for you," coaxed Bailey. She wanted to see if the horse would come to her from across the paddock. Polly swished her tail, shook her head and lowered it again. Bailey's carrot was of great interest to the other horses and the fat pony. "Okay, okay," said Bailey, breaking the carrot into five pieces. "I've got more."

Three other horses trotted over to the fence to get in on the treats. Their coats looked more shiny and they had more pep than when they arrived. All except Polly.

Bailey slipped between the fence boards and walked through the muddy clods of dirt to where Polly stood by herself. The horse twitched her ears again when Bailey softly called her name. Bailey rubbed her silky neck, then held out a chunk of carrot. Polly gently accepted it and leaned against Bailey. "That's a good girl," Bailey said. She snapped a rope lead on Polly's halter and said, "Let's go in the barn where I can groom you."

Polly plodded behind her across the paddock into the barn. Once inside, Bailey tied the lead to a circular metal ring on the wall and looked around for the currycomb. She remembered what Miss Bekka had told her: to *not* walk directly behind a horse, and to comb in the direction the hair grew, not against it. The comb was like a scrub brush with rows of rubber teeth. She started on Polly's neck, talking to her the whole time. "One of these days I'm going to ride you. Won't that be fun?"

Polly's skin rippled with pleasure from the brushing.

Goldie suddenly appeared and sat near Polly's front feet. "Be careful so you don't get kicked," said Bailey. "I'll brush you when we get home tonight." Bailey heard the barn door creak open and Miss Bekka say hello.

"What a fine job you're doing," said Miss Bekka. "You're a natural with horses. Are you sure you haven't had one in the past?"

Bailey smiled. "I want to learn everything. Like how to put the saddle and bridle on."

"And how to muck the stalls?" said Miss Bekka.

"Muck?" asked Bailey.

"Clean the manure out of them," said Miss Bekka. "It's a dirty job, but when you have a horse, it's part of it. We're all going to do it."

"Sure," said Bailey. She liked the way the barn smelled since the horses had arrived. Everything about them was new and exciting.

"Now, for some business," said Miss Bekka. "I was able to reach your mom."

Bailey stopped combing Polly. "And what did she say?"

"Molly said she thinks it's a great idea and she'll see if she can work it out with the publisher. The book isn't off press yet, but she might be able to get more bound galleys—not to sell—but to give to the first fifty or one hundred customers. She'll let us know soon."

"That would be awesome," said Bailey. Her heart was dancing. She could imagine her mom with her thick dark hair surprising Sugar and then sitting at a little table in the shop while people lined up outside the Book Barn to meet her.

Bailey would stand next to her and help out and then she and her mom and Sugar would have time alone and a special dinner. Bailey would play her clarinet for her, and she and Sugar would show how much they had learned during their piano lessons. Her mom would get to meet Goldie and Polly and everyone.

"Don't get your hopes up," Miss Bekka cautioned. "Molly's going to try to come, but it isn't definite yet."

"I know," said Bailey, "but if she can, how will we let everyone know that she's going to be here so they come to see her?"

"I think we need to make sure all the signs and posters say that there will be fantastic surprises at the grand opening. And refreshments. Everyone likes refreshments," said Miss Bekka.

"I'll help make the posters," said Bailey. She stroked Polly and reached high to comb her withers and left side. Polly shook her head.

"I've got to get back to the house. We're expecting new guests in about an hour," Miss Bekka said.

Bailey could hear Sugar calling for her. "Coming. I'll be right there," she answered loudly. She unhooked Polly's halter so that the horse was free to roam from the barn into the paddock, and put the currycomb back on the shelf.

"Thanks, Miss Bekka," she said and headed for the Book Barn, with Goldie close behind her.

21

New Guests at the Inn

"Now, which of these should go over the door?" asked Sugar, pointing at three printed cardboard signs on her work table.

Bailey read them carefully. The first had a quote from Thomas Jefferson: I CANNOT LIVE WITHOUT BOOKS. "That one's inscribed in the Library of Congress," said Sugar.

The next one read: ONCE YOU LEARN TO READ, YOU WILL BE FOREVER FREE. ~ FREDERICK DOUGLASS

And then this one: MY HOME IS WHERE MY BOOKS ARE. ~ ELLEN THOMPSON (1909)

"I know who Thomas Jefferson is, but who are the others?" asked Bailey. She unzipped her jacket and hung it on a hook by the door.

"There's a book about Frederick Douglass over there in the biography section," said Sugar. "He was a great African-American speaker and abolitionist who was against slavery. He also advised President Lincoln. I haven't been able to find anything yet about Ellen Thompson."

"I like the signs. Let's put them all up," said Bailey. "Do you need help?"

Sugar pointed to the stepladder. "Bring that over here, please, and then hand me the posters and thumb tacks."

Jefferson's quote went over the door; Douglass' over Sugar's recliner; and Thompson's over Bailey's chair.

Bailey and Sugar stood back where they could see all of them.

"Maybe we can find a good one to put above Goldie's bed," said Bailey. "I'll make one that says: 'Read to dogs. It makes them smart.' "

Goldie thumped her tail when she heard her name.

Then Bailey added, "Hey, I have an idea. We need big soft pillows near Goldie's bed so little kids can sit there and read to her."

"Good thinking," said Sugar. "It would really encourage them to practice their words."

Bailey picked up *Black Gold*, one of the horse books that Sugar had set out on her special book table. From the pictures she could see that it had something to do with horse racing. She thought about sad Polly Peachum and wondered if she'd ever be able to race with the wind. Would she even walk around without coaxing? Was Polly still standing in the barn or did she go back outside after Bailey left?

Poor Polly, thought Bailey. *I hope she feels better soon.* She decided to read the book before it was sold.

"By the way, Bekka told me new guests are arriving this afternoon," said Sugar. "I think they're a couple of musicians or artists. Bekka wasn't sure, but they like the idea of staying near a bookstore."

Bailey was only half listening. With colorful marking pens, she was making her sign to go near Goldie's bed. *The little kids will really like this,* she thought. *They'll all read to Goldie. Emily will be glad that her little brother, Howie, and their sister, Nannie, will have another place to go after school, and Justin will be happy that his sister, Fern, will have more books to read to me.*

"Time to close up for today," said Sugar. She looked at the clock. "I have three more cartons to unpack, but they can wait. Supper won't." She coughed again.

Bailey taped her sign to the wall down low where the small children could easily read it. She looked out the front window just before she closed the shade. She saw a dark green van park near the Keswicks' porch. She watched two people get out and carry small suitcases, and what looked like guitars, inside the inn.

Bailey slipped on her hooded jacket. "I'm ready," she said, tucking *Black Gold* under her arm.

22

Emily Doesn't Understand

"Are you going to try out for basketball?" asked Emily. She scooted into the seat next to Bailey. Mr. Webster closed the door and the bus became part of a long yellow line leaving the middle school parking lot. "Tournament practice starts next week. I'm going to be team captain. Didn't you tell me you know how to play?"

Bailey said, "In Florida, the kids next door had a basketball hoop in their driveway so we shot baskets sometimes."

"Then you can be on my team," said her friend. "It's after school. Mom'll give us a ride."

"I don't think so. I have to help Sugar with her bookstore," said Bailey.

"That's work," said Emily. "Aren't you going to have any fun this year?"

"The bookstore is fun," said Bailey. "I like it a lot. Plus, the horses. And I have to practice my clarinet and piano and do my homework."

"And the Keswicks. You're always doing something with them," said Emily. She scowled and pulled her dark curls into a ponytail.

"They are my friends, too," said Bailey, wishing Emily would leave her alone. She wondered if Miss Bekka had heard from her mom or if Noah and Fred had figured out the letters from the alphabet cones.

"I thought you were *my* friend. If you change your mind—" said Emily. She waited until Mr. Webster wasn't looking and quickly moved across the aisle to sit with Dona. Bailey heard her ask Dona if she wanted to be on her basketball team and Dona nodded yes.

The bus shifted gears when it turned onto Kentucky Springs Road. It slowed just before reaching Sugar's house. The driver waved to Sugar waiting in her red pickup for Bailey. Goldie's head was sticking out the window.

"What's up?" asked Bailey, gently pushing Goldie to the side as she climbed in.

"More books and treasures for the store," said Sugar, pointing to the truck bed.

"I thought you already had enough," said Bailey. "The shelves are full."

"I had another call. Someone wanted to give me all these books and I couldn't resist."

23

The Mystery Deepens

Two strangers were standing near the Book Barn's door when Sugar and Bailey came down the driveway. "They must be the inn's new guests," said Sugar. "They look like they're waiting for us to open up."

The men were tall and thin. Bailey thought they looked like brothers because they both had long stringy brown hair and noses that looked like a painting she'd seen of George Washington. Their faces seemed familiar, but Bailey decided that she was just imagining that.

"You must be Miss Sugar," said one, reaching out his hand. "I'm Milton and this is Cal Jay—we're staying at the inn while we work on new music for a concert tour."

"We're hoping you'll let us buy or borrow books during our stay," said Cal Jay, the older-looking of the two. "We read a lot when we're not practicing or composing."

"What do you play?" asked Bailey before Sugar could answer them.

Cal Jay thought for a moment, then said, "Actually, we sing and play guitar just a little. We write songs for our band called T-WagZ."

Bailey wondered if she should tell them that she played the clarinet and piano, but decided they might not be interested in that if they were really famous. She was about to go back to the truck to unload the first box of books when she saw Sugar's face. Sugar seemed puzzled as she started to unlock the door. She ran her hands over the wood around the keyhole.

"What's the matter?" asked Bailey.

"Looks like someone was trying to break in again," said her grandmother. "I can't figure this out."

"Is there a lot of crime out here?" asked Milton.

"Not usually," said Sugar.

"I'll go tell Mr. Will," said Bailey.

"Not now," said Sugar. "I don't want to worry him if everything seems to be okay inside."

She opened the door and flipped on the light. Milton and Cal Jay followed her.

"Is there anything in particular you're looking for?" Sugar asked. "We're not really open for another week."

"Just looking at the moment," said Milton.

"We do have favorite authors, but not all bookstores carry them," said Cal Jay.

"Help yourself," said Sugar. "Bailey and I have work to do."

By the time they had brought all the boxes into the little barn, the two men were carefully studying every shelf. Milton's pointer finger touched the spine of each book as if it were memorizing the author.

"Are you sure I can't help you?" called Sugar.

Cal Jay took one book off the shelf, opened it and put it back.

"Have you anything by Cowrie?" he asked.

"Books are shelved by author's name," Sugar said. "The name sounds familiar, but we've been dealing with so many books this past month I really can't remember."

Cowrie! Bailey's arms crawled with goose bumps. *I wonder why everyone wants those hollowed-out books.* She couldn't wait to finish helping Sugar so she could go find the Keswick brothers.

24

Good News

"You've got to be kidding!" said Fred. He spilled feed he was carrying to Traveller.

"And that's not all," continued Bailey. "Someone tried to break into the little barn again."

"This is just too weird," said Noah. "Let's hide the Cowrie books until we can figure out what the alphabet cone is trying to tell us."

"My book safe is hidden in my room," said Bailey, even though she didn't think anyone was likely to notice it in there.

Fred refilled the bucket and headed for the paddock. "I'm still trying to decipher the letters. They've got to mean something."

Bailey scooped sweet feed into a pan to take to Polly Peachum. Her horse looked a little perkier. She actually raised her head and sniffed the air when she heard Bailey call her name.

"Maybe when we're done with chores, we can look at the letters again," said Fred. "First, we've got to muck the stalls before Mom comes out to check on the horses." He and Noah went back into the barn.

Bailey called Polly a second time. She smiled when she saw the horse take a step toward her, and then another.

"Good girl," said Bailey softly. "Here's a special treat for you."

Polly took a few more steps, then stretched her neck and stuck her nose in the pan. Bailey held the pan very still even though she thought she heard someone walking behind her.

"Polly's doing very well. I think you should be able to get on her back soon," said Miss Bekka.

"Seriously?" asked Bailey. "I thought it might be next year."

"She's doing fine," said Miss Bekka. "Her coat is already shinier and she's gained weight. You're doing a great job with her."

"I haven't really been on a horse," said Bailey.

"Not to worry. The boys and Sparrow haven't either. Riding lessons will start for all of you, maybe as soon as this weekend after the veterinarian checks them one more time."

Bailey hugged Polly, then Miss Bekka.

"I also have news for you," said Miss Bekka.

"Have you heard from Mom?" asked Bailey, stepping backward so quickly that she bumped into her horse.

"I did. I think she's going to be able to make the grand opening," said Miss Bekka with a huge smile.

"Sweet!" said Bailey. "Sugar will be so surprised. It's going to be hard to keep the secret, though."

"I know," said Miss Bekka. "If Molly gets here early, we'll find room for her at the inn overnight. We're getting pretty full again now that those musicians arrived."

Bailey had almost forgotten about the new guests and their interest in the Cowrie books. Her mind was on seeing her mother again. She stroked Polly's warm neck. *Maybe by then I'll be able to ride my horse for her. Mom will be so amazed. And she hasn't met Goldie or the twins or Sparrow. I have so much to tell her.*

25

First Ride

Bailey raced through her Saturday chores so she could get to the Keswicks' extra early. Miss Bekka had called during breakfast to say that if it were okay with Sugar, Bailey would begin her riding lessons later in the morning.

"Slow down," said Sugar, with a laugh. "You're making me dizzy with all your running around the house. The horses aren't going anywhere."

"I've changed my bed, and picked up my clothes, and fed the cats and Goldie, and swept the porch," said Bailey out of breath. "All I have left to do is vacuum."

"And put on your shoes," said Sugar. "I think the vacuuming can wait. I'll see you at Keswicks' in about an hour after I get my desk work and calling done."

Bailey slipped into her sneakers and sweatshirt and gave Sugar a kiss on the cheek.

She bolted across the backyard, with Goldie alongside.

When she reached the Keswicks' orchard, she saw Milton and Cal Jay carrying their instrument cases down the path to the lake.

Bailey knew that even though the air was chilly when she woke up, the fall sunshine would become warm, especially at the sandy beach on Lake Anna.

She could see that Miss Bekka and Mr. Will had draped saddles on the paddock fence. Noah and Fred were cleaning them with saddlesoap while Sparrow watched.

Traveller, Sneakers, and Nelson were bridled with their reins loosely wrapped around fence posts.

"Where's Polly?" Bailey asked Noah.

"Don't worry, she's okay. Mom's putting the bridle on her now," he said.

Moments later Miss Bekka led Polly out. The horse worked her mouth around the metal bit, like she didn't like it.

"Doesn't that thing in her mouth hurt?" asked Bailey. She slid through the fence.

"No," said Miss Bekka, "not if the bit and bridle are properly adjusted and used right. It will help give you control of your horse so she knows what you want her to do. I'll show you in a few minutes."

One by one, Miss Bekka placed the saddles on the horses. She tightened the girth that went underneath each horse's belly to keep the saddle from slipping.

"Pretty soon you'll be saddling the horses yourselves," said Miss Bekka, "but that's another lesson. Now, here we go."

She motioned for Fred to come to Nelson's left side, place his left foot in the stirrup, and swing his right leg over the saddle.

"Whoops," said Fred. "This isn't easy." On the third try, he managed to perch on top. Mr. Will adjusted the stirrups to the correct length and handed Fred the reins.

"I'm not going anywhere fast, I hope," said Fred. He watched Nelson's ears twitch and the horse turned his head to see who was sitting on his back.

"Whoa. Stand still," said Fred.

Bailey thought he sounded nervous—maybe as nervous as she felt all of a sudden.

Noah was next to mount his horse. His longer legs were an advantage and it only took him two tries to get on top of Traveller. "Steady, boy," he said when Traveller walked backward a few steps.

"Now, who's next?" asked Miss Bekka.

"Me!" shouted Sparrow.

Bailey smiled. She didn't mind waiting.

Mr. Will led Sneakers to the fence, lifted Sparrow out of her wheelchair and placed her in the small saddle. Sparrow leaned down and threw her arms around the pony's neck.

"This is the almost-best day of my life," Sparrow whispered. Then she sat up and said, "I'm ready. Let's go."

"Go where?" asked Noah. "All I'm doing is going backward."

"Just a minute," said their mother. "Bailey needs to get settled on Polly." With that, she put her hands together to make a step for Bailey, then boosted her onto the saddle. Polly snorted and pawed the ground while the stirrups were being shortened. Bailey grabbed the pommel—the part of the saddle that was sticking up in front—and hung on tightly. Miss

Bekka handed her the reins and asked, "Is everyone ready?"

Bailey mumbled yes. She looked at her friends' faces and wondered if they were as afraid of falling off as she was. Polly seemed big—bigger than when Bailey stood next to her. Only Sparrow looked really happy sitting on top of her fat little pony.

Sparrow kicked Sneakers' ribs and he trotted into the center of the paddock. Sparrow bounced in the saddle, laughing as they went off.

"How do I make him turn?" she yelled.

"Pull the reins toward you in the direction you want him to go. Not too hard. Just enough to turn his head," said Miss Bekka. The pony responded and Sparrow kicked him harder to make him go even faster. All of a sudden Sneakers stopped and Sparrow had to grab on tightly to keep from falling off.

"I'm not going that fast on my first ride," said Fred.

"Watch me, bro," said Noah. He turned Traveller's head, gave him a hard nudge in the ribs, and the horse took three more steps backward, bumped into the fence and dashed for the barn door, nearly knocking Noah off as they clattered inside.

Bailey expected Fred to laugh, but he was trying to keep Nelson from following Traveller back to the stalls. Noah and his horse still hadn't returned from the barn.

To Bailey's surprise, when she nudged Polly, the horse walked forward, and turned in whatever direction Bailey decided. Bailey gained confidence with every step. The horse's slightly rocking motion was comfortable beneath her. "Good girl," Bailey said. Polly turned her ears and plodded on.

I'm doing it. I'm really riding. Bailey sat up proudly with a straight back, and leaned slightly forward just as Miss Bekka had told her to do.

26

Helping Sugar

"So, how did the first lesson go?" asked Sugar when Bailey found her in the back of the Book Barn opening the cartons of new books.

"Pretty well," said Bailey. "Miss Bekka said I look like I'm going to be a good horsewoman after a few more lessons."

"I watched you for a while and it seemed like you were having a great time. Ready for trails in the woods?" Sugar asked, coughing loudly.

"Not yet," said Bailey. "Maybe in a few weeks, after Noah and Fred . . ." She was going to say "get better at riding," but decided not to tell Sugar about all their troubles on their horses. Miss Bekka found Noah and Traveller in the horse's stall and had to help Noah down. Fred hadn't been able to move Nelson away from the barn door. Only Bailey and Sparrow had enjoyed a good first ride.

"I see you've been making posters for the grand opening," said Sugar. "They look good. But who's your surprise famous author who might be here? Is Elmo Phigg returning from Jamestown?"

Bailey's face reddened. She thought quickly. "That would be a good surprise," she said, "But I can't tell you. It's a secret."

"Just one more week and we'll be ready," said Sugar. "I'll display Mr. Phigg's books near the front door just in case. Now give me a hand with these books that go on the top shelf of the nature and wildlife section."

Bailey examined each one before she placed it on the shelf to see if it had been written by Cowrie, but there were no more.

Maybe when she met with the twins after she was done helping Sugar today they would have new ideas on what the letters from the alphabet cone shells meant.

27
Working the Puzzle

The boys were waiting for Bailey at the chicken coop. Fred had written down the letters Y O O G X T E A M on separate squares of paper and was moving them around to make different word combinations.

"All I can think of is ME GOOT LAXY," said Noah, "but that doesn't make any sense. It's funny, though."

"Try this: M AXEY," said Bailey, moving the letters again. "I wonder if that's anyone's name."

"But what about the other letters?" said Noah. "Don't we have to use all of them?"

"Just because they're on the shell doesn't mean we necessarily have to spell with them," said Bailey. "Just what makes sense."

"How about this, GO TO MAXEY," suggested Fred, moving the letters again. "Do we know of a place called Maxey?"

"I don't," said Bailey. "But what if Maxey is a person? It sounds familiar."

"If Maxey is a person, why would we need to go to him or her?" asked Fred.

"That's part of the puzzle, dude," said Noah.

Bailey stared at the letters again. "I think Maxey is an author. I think Sugar has some of his books."

"You've got to be kidding!" Fred shook his head in disbelief.

"I just can't remember what section they are in," said Bailey.

"Think hard," said Noah. "Sugar has tons of books in the store now. It would take forever to go through all of them."

"Maybe she'll remember," said Fred. "We could save time and ask her."

"Not yet," said Noah. "Let's meet in the store tomorrow after our next riding lesson. We'll start browsing."

"Okay," said Bailey. "Bring money though. If we find Maxey's books, we'll need to buy them all before someone else does."

28

E-Mail from Guam

From: pjfish2005@yermail.net>
To: "Bailey"<baileyfish@gmail.com>
Sent: 7:20 p.m.
Subject: Hi

Guess what! Dad got a job at Dahlgren and that's not far from where you stay with Sugar. He says we should be able to move there before Christmas. I can't wait to see you. I asked Mom if you could come live with us since your mother is so far away and she said she'd think about it. Dad said, "Of course." He looked really happy about my idea. Paulie and Kimo want to meet their new sister, too.

I wasn't supposed to tell you about that but I am so excited. Write me back. Norma Jean SCR

Bailey read the e-mail twice, getting angrier each time. How dare they think that she would want to live with them. A father she had met for the first time in the spring. Norma Jean, a half-sister she didn't even know about and the rest of her father's family, who lived in Guam.

I have my own mother! fumed Bailey. *I don't want to live with someone else's mother.* She slammed her hand on Sugar's computer desk. Two books slid off and thumped on the floor.

"Is everything all right?" called Sugar from the kitchen.

Bailey didn't answer. She put her head down in her arms on the desk. She felt Sugar's hands on her shoulder.

"What's the matter, dear heart?" asked Sugar softly.

Bailey pointed at the computer screen.

Sugar bent over her and silently read Norma Jean's e-mail. Bailey felt her grandmother's hands tighten.

"You seem upset," said Sugar.

"I hate them," Bailey blurted.

"I don't want you to worry," said Sugar. "Remember, I have custody while your mother is traveling. Nobody can make you go where you don't want to go." She swiveled the computer chair around so that she could cradle Bailey in her arms.

"I don't even want to see them now. Any of them," said Bailey. "Why can't they leave me alone." She held Sugar tightly.

"I think they want to get to know you better. But, we'll take one day at a time," said her grandmother. She patted Bailey on the head. "What are you going to say to Norma Jean?"

"Nothing right now," said Bailey.

"Then let's go eat," said Sugar.

29

Riding Again

Bailey felt even more confident when she sat on Polly for the second time. She was more used to the height now. She petted Polly's neck then held the reins the way Miss Bekka had shown her. Sugar watched for ten minutes, then gave her a thumbs up before going to work at the Book Barn.

Bailey trusted Polly to move when she nudged her sides with her heels, to stop when she pulled gently on the reins, and to turn in whatever direction Bailey indicated. The longer she sat in the saddle and walked Polly around the paddock, the better she felt.

Bailey looked back at the barn. Fred had managed to climb on Nelson, but Nelson still wouldn't budge. Noah was so determined to keep Traveller from going back inside that he closed the barn door before he mounted the horse.

"Watch me," said Sparrow, trotting past. She let go of the reins for a second and clapped her hands over her head.

"No tricks, young lady," said Miss Bekka, but she was smiling.

"My pony likes it," said Sparrow. "Watch this." She kicked his fat sides and Sneakers picked up the pace to a quicker trot. Polly's ears turned forward and she strained to go faster.

If Sparrow isn't afraid, then I shouldn't be, thought Bailey. She loosened the reins and nudged Polly. The horse broke into a slow bumpy trot. Bailey bounced around in the saddle.

She heard Miss Bekka calling to her. "Grip her with your knees. You need to move up and down with her. Become part of the horse. There, that's the idea."

Bailey understood and found it was more comfortable than just bouncing, which is all Sparrow cared to do.

She looked back at the boys. Nelson had finally agreed to walk around the paddock, and Traveller decided, reluctantly, to follow him, even though Nelson's tail swished in his face.

"Not fair," mumbled Noah when Bailey and Sparrow trotted past them for the fourth time.

"At least we're moving, bro," said Fred.

30

Getting Ready

Three more days to the grand opening. Bailey wondered when her mother would arrive and when she'd be able to see her.

She had finished the posters and helped Sugar tack them up around town. The last of the books were on the shelves. Sugar and Miss Bekka baked six dozen cookies and purchased cider, and the ingredients for a lemonade punch for refreshments.

Everyone had special assignments. Mr. Will and Sparrow's job was pick up helium balloons to tie on the Keswick Inn sign near the road so that customers would know where to turn for the grand opening. Noah and Fred were in charge of parking cars. Emily said she would help serve punch and cookies after her basketball game was over.

Mr. Will asked Justin if he would show people the rescue horses and the other animals.

Miss Bekka said she had invited Milton and Cal Jay to play a song or two during the afternoon and they had told her they would think about it.

Sugar would greet customers and show them around the store and Miss Bekka would help her with the sales. Mr. Will had a small table to set up just outside the front door for their surprise author.

Bailey had trouble concentrating in school on Thursday. She didn't care that she had to pound her locker three times before it opened. Friday was a day off—a teachers' work day. The timing couldn't have been better because she would be able to help Sugar more. Bailey looked at the clock.

"Write down your assignments," said Mr. Renick to the class. "We start chapter 7 on Monday."

As Bailey scooped up her books, he said, "I'll see you and your grandmother on Saturday. I think it's great that she's opening a bookstore. We need one here."

Bailey gave him a big smile.

31

Book Emergency

Bailey hoped to see a rental car in the Keswicks' parking lot and her mother's face looking out of one of the upstairs windows when she arrived at the inn after school. There was no sign, however, that Molly was there yet.

She searched Miss Bekka's face for news when she found the boys' mother helping Sugar move a display of books near the front. Miss Bekka shook her head no. Almost immediately, Miss Bekka's cell phone rang. She looked surprised and pleased and quickly went outside to talk privately.

Bailey stayed near the door, wishing she could overhear the conversation. When Miss Bekka returned she put her finger across her lips. "Your mom," she mouthed.

"What's going on?" asked Sugar. "Have you two cooked up something?"

"Oh, nothing," said Bailey.

"I just wondered if I could borrow Bailey for an hour or so early tomorrow," said Miss Bekka. "I need her help in the house."

"That'd be fine. I have to make a quick trip to the grocery store in the morning. We're short on paper cups," Sugar said, surveying the bookstore. "I think we're about ready. Looks great. Just the way I wanted it."

Bailey threw her arms around Sugar. "A lot of people are coming, including my teachers, and their kids."

"Oh, hello, Cal Jay," they heard Miss Bekka say.

"Milton and I have decided that we'd be glad to play for an hour, but we don't want to miss out on the opportunity to find our favorite authors before the other customers shop," said the man.

"May we go through the books tomorrow, even though it's just Friday?" he asked.

Miss Bekka looked at Sugar.

"I've told everyone else they have to wait, except, of course, my helpers," said Sugar.

Cal Jay shifted back and forth on his feet.

"What authors did you say you're looking for?" Sugar asked.

"Cowrie and Maxey," Milton replied. "Old family favorites."

"Cowrie sounds familiar," said Miss Bekka. "I think that's the author of one of the books that Fred bought the other day. I saw it in his room."

Oh, no! thought Bailey. *This is terrible.*

"Really!" said the man. "Most interesting. Thank you." He turned and walked briskly toward the house.

I've gotta warn Fred, thought Bailey.

"Ready to go, girl?" asked Sugar. "I'd recommend getting your homework done tonight because we will be busy at the Book Barn all weekend."

"I'll meet you at home in a minute," said Bailey. "I forgot that I have something to give to Fred."

"I'd be glad to take it to him," said Miss Bekka.

"It'll just take a minute," said Bailey, not sure what else to say.

"You might find him in the barn," said Miss Bekka. "See you in the morning."

Bailey didn't answer. She raced for the barn, afraid her feet wouldn't move fast enough.

"Fred? Fred?" she called into the shadows.

"We're over here," he said. "What's up?"

"It's an emergency," said Bailey. "That man— Cal Jay—knows about the Cowrie and Maxey books and your mom told him you had one in your room."

"She did what?" exclaimed Noah.

"She just said that she had seen it in your room. I don't think she had looked inside it."

"Here, fill the troughs with water," said Fred, handing her the hose.

He and Noah dashed from the barn for the house.

A few minutes later they returned. "One book is gone," said Fred. "I left it on a table next to my bed and now it's missing. I can't believe it!"

"I still have one in my closet," said Noah.

"One's in my room," said Bailey.

"Are you going to tell your mother?" asked Bailey.

"What's she going to do? They're guests. They'll either say they don't know anything about the book, or that they just innocently borrowed it," said Fred angrily.

"We need to keep checking the shelves before the opening to see if we missed any books by Maxey," said Noah.

"Sugar's going to town in the morning, and your mom wants me to come here for something, so maybe we can look then," said Bailey. "I don't think Sugar would mind."

32

Noah's Discovery

Sugar dropped Bailey off at the entrance to Keswick Inn on her way to the store. "I'll probably be an hour or so," she said. "I'll meet you later at the Book Barn."

"Deal!" shouted Bailey. She jogged on the carpet of leaves that had fallen on the driveway during the breezy night. Goldie kept the pace at her side.

She slowed when she reached the front steps, and looked around in confusion. Still no unfamiliar car. By now wouldn't her mother have rented one at the airport?

She knocked on the screened door, and called, "Miss Bekka?"

"In the kitchen."

Clover ran barking down the hallway, then playfully growled and grabbed Goldie's tail.

Bailey could smell more cookies baking. She envisioned her mother sitting at the kitchen table watching Miss Bekka make them while she had a big mug of hot coffee. She would jump up from her chair and grab Bailey and hold her and hold her and hold her.

But when Bailey walked in the kitchen doorway, her heart sank. Miss Bekka was alone.

Miss Bekka removed a tray from the oven and set it on a hot mat. She carefully lifted each cookie off and placed it on old newspapers to cool.

"Have one," she said to Bailey.

"I thought . . . I thought . . .," Bailey stammered.

"We both thought your mother would be here this morning. Molly called again from the road. She was afraid to arrive much before the grand opening, so she said she was staying in Richmond until early Saturday."

"Did she say how long she would be here?" asked Bailey, not really wanting to know the answer.

"The connection wasn't very good. I'm not sure." Miss Bekka slid the empty cookie sheet into the sink and came around the room until she was next to Bailey.

"I'd give you a hug, but I have a better idea. Let's use my cell phone to call your mom while Sugar's not around. Would you like that?"

Bailey nodded. Miss Bekka dialed Molly's number and handed Bailey the phone before leaving the kitchen.

"Mom? It's Bailey. . . . I can't wait to see you. . . . No, Sugar's in town for a few minutes . . . No, I need a bigger size shirt than that. . . How long will you stay? I could skip school Monday. . . . Oh, that's all? I know. . . . A surprise? . . . I love you, too. Bye."

She heard Miss Bekka coming up the back steps into the kitchen.

"Good talk?" asked Miss Bekka.

"I think she's only staying until Sunday," said Bailey. The familiar lump caught in her throat.

"Then you'll need to cram a million memories into the two days you'll have her," said Miss Bekka. "We're lucky she's able to get here at all."

Bailey looked out the kitchen window. Two days wouldn't be enough time to show her mom everything. She saw Fred and Noah waiting for her next to the Book Barn door. Bailey swallowed hard.

"Thanks for the cookie," said Bailey.

"Here, take some to the boys, too," said their mother.

~ ~ ~

"We only have a couple of minutes," said Bailey, handing cookies to Noah and Fred. She walked to the side of the little barn and lifted the spare key off a nail. She unlocked the shop's door and she and the boys went inside.

"Let's lock it," said Noah, "so no one can come in." The lock clicked when he turned the knob.

"Where do we begin?" asked Fred. He wiped his glasses on his windbreaker and stared at the thousands of books now on the shelves.

"You look in the Florida section, and I'll look in nature and shells," said Bailey.

"I'll look in fiction in case Sugar organized the books by author there," said Noah.

"Don't mess up anything," warned Bailey. "We have to leave it the way Sugar has it."

She searched the shelling books first for Cowrie, then for Maxey. "Nothing here," she said.

"I didn't find anything in the Florida section, either," said Fred. "I've also looked in other state sections, such as North Carolina, Connecticut, Texas and Virginia."

"Wait a minute," said Noah. "I didn't see anything by Maxey, but I found this by M. Axey." He carefully removed the thick volume, and shook it. "Listen," he said. "Something rattles."

"Open it!" said Fred.

Noah lifted the cover. "Wow!" he exclaimed.

Just then there was a loud knocking on the door.

"Quick, hide the book," said Fred.

Noah looked around. "Where?"

"Under Goldie's bed," Bailey said.

Noah hurried across the room and slid the book under the tan dog bed. The knocking continued until a key turned in the lock.

33

Secret Inside

"I've been looking all over for you," said Miss Bekka. "What's going on? Are you supposed to be doing something for Sugar in here?"

"We were trying to find another Cowrie book—you know, the author that Cal Jay wants," said Noah.

"That's thoughtful. Did you find one?" asked his mother.

"No," said Noah. "So, I guess we're done in here, right, bro?" He looked at Fred.

"Good," said Miss Bekka. "I need help in the yard. I want you to take stakes and mark the parking area for the grand opening in the field. I don't want people driving through the gardens by mistake."

"Sure, Mom," said Fred. "We'll do it."

"I'm going to see Polly," said Bailey, breathing a sigh of relief that Miss Bekka's questions had stopped.

She hoped that Miss Bekka would leave first, giving them a chance to grab the book, but the boys' mother waited until Noah, Fred and Bailey stepped outside before locking the door behind them.

As soon as she went back to the house, Noah muttered, "We couldn't get the book, but at least it's safely hidden for now."

"What's inside it?" asked Bailey.

"You'll never guess."

"Tell me," she said.

"I'll have to show you," he said with a grin. "There's photograph of an old man bending over on a beach and also a scrap of paper with part of a map," said Noah.

"A map of what?" asked Bailey.

"It looked like part of Florida," said Noah, "or maybe Alabama."

"That doesn't make any sense," said Fred.

"None of it does," said Noah.

34

Grand Opening

"Oh, no!" Bailey exclaimed when she looked out her dormer window. "It can't rain. It just can't rain today."

The sky was gloomy with storm clouds.

Rats! It absolutely can't rain today, she thought, quickly dressing. She pulled on her red sweatshirt that had SUGAR'S BOOK BARN printed on it. Sugar had given similar sweatshirts and T-shirts to everyone who would be helping with the grand opening and working at the store. Even Goldie had a red scarf with the store's name printed on it. "Good advertising," Sugar had said.

Bailey found Sugar in the kitchen reading the morning paper. She didn't look concerned about the weather.

"What if it rains?" Bailey asked.

"A rainy day might bring more customers," said Sugar, cheerfully. "They'll postpone apple or pumpkin picking in favor of an indoor activity." Sugar took another sip of coffee. "And we'll move the surprise author's table inside."

I wonder if Mom is there yet? I hope she's not late, worried Bailey. She finished the last of her scrambled eggs.

"Ready?" asked Sugar. "This is a pretty exciting day. We'll take the truck just in case it pours."

Bailey and Goldie climbed into the pickup. A few drops splattered on the windshield. There was still no unfamiliar car at Keswick Inn.

Where could she be? Maybe she isn't coming after all. Bailey's heart was as heavy as a loaded book bag.

Sugar unlocked the shop, turned on the lights and the OPEN sign. She smiled and looked around. "A dream come true," she said. "I've always wanted to have my own bookstore. You know, Bailey, sometimes it takes a while to make dreams happen, but it's never too late, even when you get to be my age."

"You're not old, Sugar," said Bailey. She threw her arms around her grandmother.

"I'm sure not as young as I used to be," said Sugar, hugging back.

"Me neither," said Bailey, laughing.

"Now we have to see if we have customers," said Sugar. She ran her fingers through her hair.

Bailey looked out a window and watched Miss Bekka pop open a green umbrella. She dashed across the yard with a large plastic container. The bells on the door tinkled as she pushed it open with her foot. "Hadn't expected the rain this morning," Miss Bekka said breathlessly. "It's supposed to clear by noon, though. Here are the first of the refreshments. The boys will bring the rest in a few minutes."

Miss Bekka and Sugar spread out a heavy woven tablecloth on a table near the door. Sugar placed a centerpiece with orange and yellow dried flowers in the middle.

"Cookies at this end and the punch bowl over there," Sugar said.

The door's bells tinkled again. "The punch bowl goes where?" asked a familiar voice.

"Mom!" shouted Bailey. "You made it!" She sprang across the room and grabbed her.

"Molly, what on earth? What are you doing here?" asked Sugar. She was so surprised she spilled a stack of plastic cups.

"I'm your special guest," Molly said. "I don't have a punch bowl, but I have seventy-five copies of my bound galley to autograph and give away to your customers. Hope that's okay."

"Okay? This is an incredibly wonderful surprise," said Sugar.

"Great shop," said Molly, stroking Bailey's hair. "Should keep you plenty busy, although you are plenty busy already, taking care of our girl, aren't you, Sugar?"

Molly lifted Bailey's face up and said, "I can't believe how much you've grown, girlfriend, since I last saw you in the spring." When Molly pushed her thick brown hair back, Bailey had a glimpse of her engagement ring. It was bigger than Bailey had expected. She pretended not to notice it.

"Now, where should I set up my table?" asked Molly. She hugged Bailey again.

"How about over here. We can move the dog's bed," said Sugar.

"I'll do it," said Bailey. Before anyone else could reach the large soft pillow, she pulled Goldie off. She then felt around under the big cushion, found the book and slid it under a navy bean bag chair in the children's section. She dragged the dog bed near the window. Goldie followed and flopped down on it.

"That's my dog, Goldie," she said to her mom. "You can pet her. She likes it a lot."

"Oh dear," said Molly. The bells tinkled again. "Andrew's so allergic. I'm afraid to get her fur on my clothes. I had no idea the dog would be in the store."

Andrew? Dr. Andrew Snorge-Swinson. Bug Man. Here? Bailey looked at the man with a ponytail coming through the door with a large carton of books.

"Where do you want these?" he said with a smile for Sugar.

"Andrew. My goodness. Another surprise," Sugar said. "I guess you can set them down behind my desk."

He sneezed. "Good to see you," said Bug Man, sneezing again. "And how are Sugar and Bailey?"

Bailey stepped backwards toward the window and politely said, "Hello, Dr. Snorge-Swinson." She sheltered the tail-wagging dog with her arms.

Bug Man's ponytail bounced when he sneezed loudly and he blew his nose in a large handkerchief. His eyes were watery behind his thick glasses.

"Maybe the dog can go outside," said Molly. "You know that Andrew has terrible allergies to animals."

"But, Mom," said Bailey, "Goldie is always in the Book Barn with us. Besides, it's raining. She can't stay out there." She looked at Sugar

133

for backup. Sugar looked perplexed. Bug Man sneezed hard three times.

"Let's take her home. It will be just for a little while, Bailey," said her grandmother. "Goldie won't mind."

"I'll drive her," said Miss Bekka.

Bailey flushed. She took Goldie by the collar and walked her close to Bug Man on the way to Miss Bekka's van. She hoped some of Goldie's hair would get on his clothes so he would sneeze for days, maybe weeks.

Miss Bekka patted Bailey on the shoulder when they were both outside. "Remember, this is your grandmother's day. We need to make it a happy one," she said.

But what about me? thought Bailey.

35

Bad News

Cal Jay, Milton, and the woman with the husky voice were the first customers. They silently and carefully searched the shelves, shaking their heads in disappointment in each aisle.

"The dog bed's moved," said Noah, when he came in the store with a second container of cookies. "Where's the book?"

"I had to hide it again," whispered Bailey. "Don't talk about it now. They might hear us."

"Your mom seems real nice," said Fred. "So does that dude she's going to marry."

Bailey gave him a look that said don't talk about that either. Her mother looked prettier and happier than she could ever remember.

Molly greeted customers who came through the door, talked about her book and about Dr. Andrew Snorge-Swinson, and she used a pen with bright green ink to sign her name in the galleys.

Bug Man had pulled up a chair next to hers and answered questions about his work with insects in Costa Rica. Even Cal Jay, Milton and the tall woman talked with Molly and Bug Man on their way out.

"Sure, I know of Cowrie," Bailey heard Bug Man say. "Interesting work on shells."

Sugar was right. Customers sloshed across the muddy yard and into the store all morning. By noon, Molly was out of galleys and was simply signing her name on pieces of paper. Bug Man also signed his name. "I'm sure Sugar will carry the finished book when it is out in January," Molly told people.

"Come take a break from the cash register, Bailey," Molly said. "I need to hold you again."

Bailey stood awkwardly next to her mother, wishing that Bug Man would go outside, even if it was pouring, so she could have time alone with her mom. Her mother pulled her down into her lap. "Be my baby for a minute," Molly said. "Just like you used to be." Molly turned to Andrew. "For eleven years it was just Bailey and me, and now there will be the three of us, plus your kids when they visit."

Bailey jumped up, her face red. "What do you mean?"

"I mean, we'd like you to live with us after the wedding, maybe sooner. Andrew's divorced, also, and has two boys in California. They're in high school," Molly continued. She didn't seem aware of how upset Bailey had become.

"I'm not going anywhere," said Bailey.

"Shhh. Not so loud," said Molly. "Hello, there, I'm Molly Fish," she said cheerfully to Mr. Renick and his wife, who were shaking off raincoats at the door.

The Renicks' four-year-old son made a beeline to the children's section, where he picked up *Babar* and flopped down in the navy beanbag chair.

Oh, no! thought Bailey. *I've got to move the book.*

"This chair is lumpy," said the boy. He lifted up the corner and pulled out the book. "No pictures," he said and shoved it hard across the floor. The book slid under the kids' table.

Noah, who had been watching, ducked under the table at the same time as Bailey did.

"Now what do we do?" she whispered.

"I'll take it and get it out of here," he said.

36

Bug Man and Bailey

"Phew! What a great day," said Sugar when she turned off the OPEN sign. "We sold at least 150 books." She sat in her recliner and put her feet up. "Have a seat."

Molly sat at Sugar's desk and Andrew settled in the other recliner—Bailey's. Bailey scrunched down at the toddler table.

"Sugar, you look tired, and I don't like that cough," said Molly. "Are you sure, at your age, that you're feeling up to running a store?"

"Yes, indeed. My cold is almost gone and I've got good help. It's just been a busy time getting everything ready. I'm so glad that you'll be able to be with us tomorrow. We can spend the day relaxing," Sugar said.

Molly turned her head toward Andrew. "I had hoped we could stay, but I just learned that we need to leave after supper to get to New York. We have one final meeting with the publisher's people before the book comes out in January."

"So soon? That's too bad. I'd hoped for a longer visit," said Sugar, looking at Bailey as if she expected her to agree. Bailey said nothing.

Dr. Snorge-Swinson cleared his throat. "Molly and I are hoping that Bailey will join us in Costa Rica . . ."

"It wouldn't be until after Christmas," interrupted Molly, "maybe even later, depending on when the publisher plans a book tour for us."

Sugar looked like she had been given bad-tasting medicine. She glanced at Bailey, then stood up and said, "This is rather sudden. A surprise. We weren't expecting . . . but then . . . Bailey is your child." Sugar suppressed a cough.

"That's right," said Molly. "We want to be a family—again."

"I'm not going anywhere," said Bailey. She knocked over the toddler table when she jumped to her feet. She surprised herself with how determined she sounded. She had wanted her mom's visit to be wonderful, but instead it had turned into a terrible idea.

Molly's smile faded. "Bailey!" she said sharply. "What's the matter with you?"

Bailey said nothing but planted her feet next to Sugar's.

"Perhaps I should leave you three alone to talk," said Andrew.

"No, stay," said Molly. "You're also part of my life. We'll work this out together."

"I think you and I need to have a conversation," Sugar said to Molly. "Let's go in the storage room."

When they disappeared into the back of the store, Bailey found herself alone with Bug Man.

"I'm sorry our news hasn't made you happy," said Dr. Andrew Snorge-Swinson. "I know we would like each other if we had a chance. And I know you'll love Costa Rica. It's a beautiful country with excellent schools." His eyes watered and he sneezed again.

Bailey shifted back and forth on her feet. She didn't care what he thought about her.

"I'm going home to feed *my cats* and *my dog*," Bailey finally said. "I would never move anywhere without them."

Before he could respond, she slipped on her yellow slicker and ran out into the rain.

37

Lost in Thought

The phone rang shortly after Bailey had fed her pets. It was her grandmother calling from the Book Barn.

"Hurry back, sweetheart," said Sugar. "We're going out for supper before your mom and Andrew leave."

"What'd she say?" asked Bailey.

"We'll talk later," said Sugar.

Bailey slowly hung up the phone. She didn't feel like eating or visiting with anyone. Her mother would want a new picture of Bailey, herself and probably Bug Man to take back to with them. She would want Bailey to smile and look happy. That wasn't how Bailey felt.

Bailey made sure she had lots of dog and cat hair on her sweatshirt even though she knew that wasn't very nice. She wanted Bug Man to sneeze so hard that he would land back in the rain forest. "You have to stay here, girl," she said to Goldie. The hound whined and tried to sneak out with her. Bailey quickly shut the door. Goldie barked sharply as Bailey walked across the porch and down the steps.

The rain had finally let up. Red and yellow leaves glistened on the ground and squished when she stepped on them. The storm brought a frosty drop in temperature. Bailey shuddered at the cold, wishing she had worn a warm jacket over her sweatshirt. She blew on her hands and shoved them in her jeans pockets. She missed Goldie running alongside her to Keswick Inn. A lump in her throat that started in the afternoon was getting larger. If it was just Mom, that would be okay. But Mom *and* Bug Man and his kids? Never!

Bailey picked up a stick in the path and hurled it into the woods. She heard it crack when it thumped against a tree. She looked for another one, not caring that her hair was getting wet from water dripping off the branches overhanging the path. She kicked a rock into the small stream gushing from the storm.

Beyond the stream was a large log about ten feet back in the woods and well hidden by holly bushes. Bailey pushed through the branches and sat down on the log even though it was damp and cold.

She was in no hurry to return to the Book Barn although she knew everyone was waiting for her.

She heard people calling her name as the shadows deepened. She shivered. *I wish Goldie were here,* she thought. A wave of sadness swept over her until she felt like she couldn't breathe.

 Bailey buried her face in her hands. Cold drops from a sycamore tree dribbled down her neck.

38

Gone

A cold wet nose nudged Bailey's face. She opened her eyes and flung her arms around Goldie. "How did you get here, girl?" Bailey whispered.

"I knew she'd find you," said Fred. "Where have you been? Everyone's looking for you. They were really worried when you didn't come back."

"Sorry," said Bailey. "I forgot what time it was."

"I found her!" Fred shouted. "I found her!"

Bailey could hear voices respond to his call. She stood up. Her jeans were wet from sitting on the log. She pushed her damp hair behind her ears.

"This way," said Fred. His flashlight pointed in the direction of the inn.

"It's none of my business but are you mad at your mother?" he asked. He turned and looked at Bailey for an answer. She didn't know what to say.

"It's okay. You don't have to say anything," Fred said. "I overheard what she said about taking you away from here. I didn't like that either." He kept walking but turned for another quick glance.

"And I didn't like Bug Man—well, not very much. He's an interesting dude, but he sneezed when he saw Clover looking out my bedroom window," Fred continued.

Bailey had to smile at that. She petted Goldie's head.

Within moments they were in the clearing and through the orchard. The porch light was on and Bailey could see Sugar and the rest of the Keswicks following the flashlight's beam across the yard, past the big barn and the Book Barn.

Sugar hurried down the steps and ran across the yard. She smothered Bailey with a hug.

"You had us so worried," Sugar said. Bailey realized tears were running down her grandmother's cheeks.

"I'm sorry," Bailey said quietly. "I didn't mean to worry anyone."

"C'mon inside," said Mr. Will. "Bailey needs to dry off and warm up by the fire."

Bailey blinked in the bright hall light.

"Where's Mom?" she asked.

"They had to go. It was getting very late and they had a train to catch, remember?" said Sugar, with a frown.

"She left without saying good-bye?"

"I think *you left* without saying good-bye," said Sugar. "Molly was quite upset."

Bailey slumped in a chair near the fire.

"I've screwed up everything," she said. "This was supposed to be a special day for you and I've ruined it."

She looked around the room. Everyone had tiptoed out to give Bailey and Sugar privacy.

Sugar pulled up a chair next to Bailey's knees so that she could look into her granddaughter's face.

They gazed silently at each other. Bailey couldn't remember ever feeling so terrible. She had let everyone down.

Finally Sugar smiled and said, "I love your mother dearly. However, she's impulsive and adventurous and doesn't always think through the consequences."

Bailey looked puzzled.

"From the time she was little, Molly would dash off in this direction or that, forgetting her shoes, or that it was a school day instead of a

Saturday. I often worried about her. Then, for a while, she seemed to settle down, especially after she had you. But, the itch for adventure started again, and off she went to Costa Rica," said Sugar.

"And she met Bug Man," said Bailey.

"Yes, she met Andrew," said Sugar. "He's not all bad—a rather interesting fellow—but I can understand that you wouldn't like him—at least not now."

"I won't like him ever," said Bailey.

"What I don't like," Sugar continued, "is the way your mother expects you and me to be happy about her plans, the plans that she's excited about."

Bailey looked intently into her grandmother's eyes.

"She doesn't seem to be considering our feelings," said Sugar, "because she's so excited about her book and getting married." Sugar coughed, but not as badly as she had in the morning.

Bailey said, "That's all she thinks about. Her plans."

Sugar leaned forward. "When we had our talk, that's basically what I told her. I said that it wasn't fair to move you again in the middle of a school year if you didn't want to go, and that she shouldn't try to make you like Andrew.

Even though she thinks I'm too old to be run a business, I said that I have an excellent helper and I wasn't about to give you up anytime soon."

"You did?" said Bailey. "You said that?"

"I did. Plus, I told her that you and I would come to Costa Rica for a visit together—maybe next summer—if you decide to stay here."

Bailey's mind was in a jumble. "What'd she say?"

"Molly thought about it and we talked some more and then she said okay. She wanted to tell you herself that we had worked things out, but you were gone. We decided it's up to you what you want to do. You're old enough to decide."

The lump returned to Bailey's throat. She had run away instead of talking it out as her mother had always told her to do when there were problems. Now she could choose to stay at the lake with Sugar, her pets and friends, but that might hurt her mother's feelings. *I don't know what to do!* Bailey thought.

"Sweetheart, don't look so sad. Your mom and Andrew will stop by again in a few days before they go back, so you'll have a chance to talk with them about whatever you decide. It's all up to you. Meanwhile, Miss Bekka has planned a special supper in honor of the grand opening. Let's celebrate," said Sugar.

39

Next Guess

Bailey stretched out under her covers and pulled the heirloom red, white and blue quilt under her chin. Goldie was already hogging the bed and Sallie and Shadow had left Bailey only a small part of her pillow.

Bailey thought about her mother. She would try to make it up to her—to them—when they returned. While her mother and Bug Man were traveling, she planned to read Molly's galley about him and would ask him about his sons.

She'd tell them she'd come visit them next summer, if she decided to stay with Sugar at least for a while.

Bailey still wasn't sure what she should do. What she *should* do and what she *wanted* to do were very different. Her mom hadn't given her a choice about leaving Florida and her friends and moving to Virginia in the winter. Now, it was completely up to her. Bailey sighed. She loved her mom, but nothing was the same anymore. And she loved Sugar, who was always there for her, and being here with her new friends. And how could she leave Goldie, Shadow, Sallie, and Polly? This was so hard.

Bailey turned her head and looked at the bright blue T-shirt with pictures of Costa Rican shells on it that her mom had brought for her. It was a size too small, but maybe she could squeeze into it when her mom returned.

Shells. What about the mystery of the alphabet cone shells? And why were Milton, Cal Jay and that strange woman searching for books by Cowrie and M Axey or Maxey?

If Bailey hadn't spent so much time in the woods she could have asked her mother to help solve the mystery.

Bailey tried to get comfortable as she thought again about the mysterious letters. M Axey. Maxey. My Axe.

My Axe. There was a combination they hadn't thought of before, but what could it mean? Bailey's eyes opened wide. Wait until I tell the twins, she told Goldie, who was snoring between her feet.

40

Getting Closer

On grand opening Sunday, the Book Barn opened at noon. Bailey and Goldie rode with Sugar in the pickup. The Keswicks's driveway had several large muddy puddles that sprayed reddish water over the bumper and tires.

Even though it was only 11:40 A.M., a car was parked near the bookstore door and Bailey saw three people talking under a tree. Fred and Noah came out of the big barn and walked over to Sugar's store.

While Sugar unlocked the door, Bailey pulled her friends aside. "We've got to find a book called *My Axe*. I saw it in there somewhere. I think it'll help us solve the mystery."

"You don't know which section?" asked Noah. He unzipped his jacket.

"No. I can't remember. C'mon."

The bells tinkled as she shut the door behind them and tinkled again when Cal Jay,

Milton, and the strange woman followed them inside.

"What are they doing here?" whispered Fred.

"Hurry," answered Bailey. "We've got to find the book before they do."

She, Fred and Noah started down separate aisles. She heard her grandmother greet the customers, and say, "No, I don't keep a listing of titles or authors. You'll just have to peruse the shelves. I'll have some hot cider ready in a minute if you care to join me."

The books were organized alphabetically by author, but Bailey had no idea who had written *My Axe*. Maybe that wasn't even the right book, but they had to find out. Nothing else had made sense.

Bailey hoped her grandmother wouldn't need help with anything so that she would have time to hunt for the book. Bailey didn't think it would be in the children's section. She knew it wasn't among the shell or nature books.

Fred passed by her and whispered, "I've checked tools and camping. Nothing there."

Noah shook his head after he finished looking through historical fiction and biographies.

Bailey's heart pounded every time she saw the three customers take a book off the shelf.

What if they find it first? What are they looking for? She could smell the hot cider with cinnamon brewing near the front of the store.

She reached for a wooden stool so that she could get a closer look at the books on the top shelf of the autobiographies.

To her amazement, there it was: *My Axe, a Musical Life* by Oliver Shelby Cowrie.

Just as she pulled it toward her, a large hand reached up and snatched the book. Bailey lost her balance and wobbled off the stool.

"Found it," Milton said to his companions. "At last."

41

Ready to Tell

"That's my book," said Bailey loudly from where she had landed on the floor. "I had it first."

"Be quiet, child. I think your grandmother will sell it to us," said Cal Jay. "We're paying customers." He tried to head toward the cash register, but Fred and Noah blocked his way.

"Give it back," hissed Fred. "Bailey had it first."

Milton gave him a stony look. "We'll see about that. It belongs to our family."

"Cider's ready," called Sugar from her refreshment table near the front door.

For a moment, no one moved. Then Milton tried to push the boys aside.

Goldie suddenly jumped from her bed and barked. Bailey, for once, didn't try to make her stop. The dog came down the aisle and blocked Milton and Cal Jay from making their way to the front of the store.

"Goldie, hush!" scolded Sugar. Then she saw Bailey's red face. "What on earth is going on here?"

Bailey decided it was time to say something. She looked at Fred and Noah. They nodded. "Sugar, we need your help. They are trying to take books that belong to us and weird things are happening," said Bailey.

Sugar looked puzzled. She placed her hands on her hips. "What do you mean? You know we shouldn't accuse people . . ."

Bailey took a deep breath. "Milton grabbed that book out of my hand," said Bailey. "They are trying to get all the hollow books we bought."

"One is even missing from my room," said Fred. He glared at Milton. "I think you have it."

"Hollow books? I didn't know we had any. What's special about them?" asked Sugar.

"They're mostly by the same author and they're book safes," said Noah. "They have things in them."

"What kinds of things?" Sugar was clearly perplexed. "What authors?"

"Cowrie and M Axey or Maxey. They contain shells, letters, a photograph and even part of a map," said Noah.

Fred added, "But we found them first and these people are trying to take them away."

"I really must know what's going on," said Sugar, looking hard at the two men.

"Okay," said Milton. "Perhaps you deserve an explanation, but only after the kids show us the other book safes. I know you have them all. We must see them as a group."

Milton clutched *My Axe* to his chest. "These books must be kept together," he said softly, then sighed. "You have no idea how important this collection is to us."

"Please go get all of them," said the tall woman, who had come up behind Bailey, "and then we'll tell you everything."

"Yes, I think you should," said Sugar, "and it better be a good story or I will call the sheriff." She pulled her cell phone out of her pocket. "Frankly, I need to have a look at all the books, but remember that they have already been purchased by my helpers. You may not have any of them unless they agree to sell." She nodded at Bailey and the boys, "Now, please get the book safes."

"Meanwhile, we'll help ourselves to your grandmother's cider," said Cal Jay. He tapped Fred on the arm. I think you'll find your book safe has returned to your bedside table."

"We'll be back in a few minutes," Bailey said to Sugar. She and the boys hurried outside.

"What's all this about?" asked Fred.

"I have no idea," said Bailey. Goldie raced with her down the path to the woods.

42

Opening the Book

Bailey's copy of *Angel Wings at Dawn* was exactly where she had left it on her desk. She made sure the alphabet cone shell was inside and hurried back to the Book Barn. Noah and Fred were already inside with their copies of the book safes.

"She's back," said the strange woman. She tossed her empty cup in a nearby trash can. "Let's spread things out on this table. Do you mind if we move your books aside?"

"I guess not," said Sugar, helping push the copies of her favorites closer to the cash register. Fred and Noah brought folding chairs from the back room so that there were enough seats for everyone.

"It's a long story," said Milton, "and one that goes back to our childhood. We're cousins. This is Oliva. We grew up in the same town and often spent time visiting our grandparents."

"Our grandfather, Oliver Shelby Cowrie, was famous for many things. He collected rare shells, played the saxophone and guitar, wrote books, and played tricks on us," offered Cal Jay.

"My, he must have been fun to be around," said Sugar, blowing on her cup of cider to cool it.

"It was fun for a while, but then he told us he had a puzzle for us to figure out, and it would lead us to a treasure," said Oliva in her husky voice.

"What sort of treasure?" asked Noah.

"A rare family treasure is all we knew," said Cal Jay. "We've been guessing and following his clues and maps for years. Every once in a while, Grandfather—that's a picture of him on the beach—would give us another hint—usually when we visited him during the holidays. On the last time, he told us that books contained the greatest treasures of all."

Oliva said, "That led us to books authored by him, and we realized that he had created book safes that contained clues, including maps, word puzzles, the special shells, and alphabet cones, which he collected when he visited Florida from his home in Georgia."

"He wanted us to use our brains to follow the clues," said Cal Jay.

Oliva continued, "Once we figured out that the clues were in books with shell names in the title, we began searching for everything he wrote. The trail recently led us to a used-book store in Culpeper, but just before we were able to buy them, the store closed and we had to find out who had purchased all the books by Cowrie." She nodded in Sugar's direction.

"But what does this have to do with *My Axe*?" Bailey asked. "That book was in the music section, not in with the shells."

"Good question," said Milton, still clutching *My Axe*. "The joke is that 'axe' is a slang name for both the jazz saxophone and guitar, which he played. We're hoping this book contains the family treasure that we've been looking for all these years."

Milton carefully placed *My Axe* in the center of the table.

Bailey scraped her chair on the floor as she pushed herself closer.

There was a hush in the shop. Sugar finally said, "Aren't you going to open it?"

"Hurry up, Cousin, we haven't got all day," said Oliva.

Milton lifted the cover and peered inside. He looked surprised. He took out a small, bulging red velvet sack that was tied closed with a black ribbon. Inside was a yellowed envelope. Milton held it in his trembling palm. He paused, as if after all these years of searching for the treasure, he was afraid to open it.

43

Treasure

"If you won't open it, then I will," said Oliva. She snatched the envelope from Milton's hand.

"Don't tear it. Be careful," urged Cal Jay.

Sugar reached for a letter opener on her desk and handed it to Oliva.

The woman slid the blade into the top of the envelope and quickly sliced it open. She turned the envelope upside down and out dropped three large gold coins and a folded piece of paper.

"It's in Grandfather's handwriting," Oliva said. "You read it." She handed the paper back to Milton. He studied it for a moment, looked slowly around the table at his cousins, then Sugar, Bailey and the boys. For the first time since Bailey had seen the new guests at the inn, Milton's eyes were burning with excitement.

"I hope Grandfather isn't up to his old tricks," he said. He read:

My dear young grandchildren—When you find this note, I will be long gone. I hope the clues have led you on a magnificent search in and out of bookstores and libraries. I hope you have learned much as you've discovered the treasures books contain—new words, new ideas, adventures, mind-bending information. There is nothing quite like books.

That is my treasure for you—to make you readers. To make you smart.

I am also giving you each a gold coin as your reward, and I hope you do something special with them.

With great affection, Grandfather

"There you have it!" Sugar said, breaking the silence around the table. The mystery is solved; the treasure revealed." She waited for the cousins to speak.

The Cowrie cousins picked up their coins and studied them with curiosity, then frowns.

"A prankster to the end," grumbled Milton. "These coins are fake. They are souvenirs from a pirate festival in Tampa." He skidded his coin across the table toward *My Axe.*

"What are we going to do now?" asked Cal Jay. He tossed his coin back in the book safe. "What a waste of effort. All these years for nothing," he complained.

Oliva didn't answer. She simply pocketed her coin, then stood up to leave.

"Let's put these unusual books on display in the front of the store," suggested Sugar. "I think visitors will find their story interesting, and," she paused, "will be inspired to learn more about shells and maybe even music."

"Keep them," mumbled Milton.

The door tinkled as the Cowrie cousins left the book safes behind and stomped into the chilly afternoon air.

"Good-bye," Sugar called after them. "Do come again." She laughed without coughing for the first time in days.

44

Decision

At closing time, Sugar turned out the lights and locked the Book Barn door.

"I suspect the Cowrie cousins may have had something to do with trying to pry open the shop door," she said to Bailey. "Given their huffy reaction, it just shows you that they had missed the real treasure in the Book Barn—the priceless value of books."

Bailey grinned and said, "Mind if I go to the big barn before we go? I haven't spent much time with Polly in a couple of days."

"I'll go with you," said her grandmother. "I need to get to know my steed, Old Baldy, now that I'm feeling better."

Bailey turned on the lights near the stalls and walked with Goldie to the fourth one on the left. "Polly? Hey, Polly," she said quietly. She leaned over the wooden door. Polly's nose was in a water bucket near the window.

Bailey called her name again and looked around for a pan to fill with sweet feed.

Polly's ears pricked. Water dribbled from her muzzle as she lifted her head. She snorted when she saw Bailey, turned and ambled over to the stall door. Polly stretched her neck over the boards until her check was next to Bailey's face. Bailey held out the shallow dish with feed and Polly's tongue tasted her favorite treat.

Bailey stroked Polly's white blaze and brushed the mare's forelock out of her eyes.

The horse no longer looked droopy. Her coat had a shine and her ribs were barely visible.

Bailey said softly, "Polly, we're going to have lots of adventures when I'm better at riding. And, guess what? I'll going to be around for a long time." The words unexpectedly spilled out of Bailey's mouth. They sounded right.

Just then Bailey heard familiar humming. Polly's ears twitched and she looked in the direction of Old Baldy's stall. Bailey turned her head slightly. "I'll be around," she said louder to make sure that Sugar could hear. "I've made up my mind. I'm staying, if that's okay."

Sugar's face lit with a huge smile and she said, "Of course it's okay! Stay as long as you want, Bailey, dear. Now, let's go home. We have work to do, books to read, and lots of adventures to plan."

Discussion Questions

1. Why does Bailey give her copy of her mother's book away? To whom does she give it? What are her feelings about the book? What makes her sad/angry about her mother's bio on the last page?

2. Pretend you are Bailey and write an e-mail to your friend Amber in Florida. Tell her how you feel about Bug Man and why. Tell her what you think it would be like if your mom married Bug Man and you had to live with them. What would the house look like?

3. When the mysterious customer comes into the Sugar's bookstore the first time, what did you think she was looking for? What did you think, at first, was hidden in the Cowrie books?

4. If you had been Bailey and alone when the mysterious customer came back, how would you have gotten her to leave? Why did she leave?

5. Bailey has the idea of having her mother come to Sugar's bookstore opening as a surprise. Did you think Miss Bekka would be able to convince her to come?

6. Ambivalent means feeling two ways at the same time. Why does Bailey feel ambivalent about her mom coming to sign books at the Book Barn opening?

7. Bailey has fantasies about exactly what it will be like when her mother returns for the Book Barn opening. Did you think those dreams would come true? Why or why not?

8. At the first riding lesson, Fred is pretty nervous and Bailey is excited. How do you feel about trying new things? How much does your confidence depend on who is teaching you? Is Miss Bekka a good teacher? Why or why not? What makes a teacher someone you can trust?

9. Miss Bekka is rescuing horses. Find out about other animals that are in shelters and need adoption near where you live.

10. Norma Jean, Bailey's half-sister, writes that their dad, Paul, and his second family are moving closer to Sugar and Bailey. If you were Bailey would you want to live with Molly and Bug Man, Paul and his new family, or Sugar? Give three reasons for your choice.

11. Why do you think Sparrow is the first to become a good horseback rider?

12. How did you think Cal Jay and Milton might be connected to the mysterious shopper? Give two reasons why you were suspicious of them.

13. Why do you think Bailey got so upset when her mom says she would like Bailey to live with her and Bug Man after the wedding? How does Sugar react to this invitation/news?

14. What does Sugar tell Bailey after Molly and Andrew leave? Did part of Bailey and Sugar's conversation surprise you? Should Sugar have told Bailey these things about Molly?

15. What treasure was in the final book safe? What lesson did Grandfather Oliver want Oliva, Milton and Cal Jay to learn? How do they react to the surprise their grandfather left to them? What is the real treasure?

16. Are treasures always worth a lot of money? Do you have any treasures that would not be worth much if you tried to sell them, but are very valuable to you anyway? Do you have any treasures that are not even "things"? If the treasure was a gift, write about the person who gave it to you.

17. Were you surprised by Bailey's choice? Did you agree with her decision?

Web Sites

http://www.shellmuseum.org/

http://www.foldingguides.com/PDFs/
Seashelltreasures25.pdf

http://americanhistory.suite101.com/article.cfm/
rare_facts_about_george_washington

http://wiki.Monticello.org/mediawiki/index.php/
Horses

http://gwpapers.virginia.edu/projects/faq/
govern.html

http://library.thinkquest.org/J0112391/
frederick_douglass.htm

http://www.findagrave.com/cgi-bin/
fg.cgi?GRid=3082&page=gr

*(Sites are available as of press time. Author and
publisher have no control of material or links to
other sites.)*

From Sugar's Book Barn

Alphabet Cones: Living, Learning Tools, (brochure) Harlan Wittkopf

Beach Treasures of the Gulf Coast, Harlan Wittkopf and Peter Dance

Black Beauty, Anna Sewell

Black Gold, Marguerite Henry

Brighty of the Grand Canyon, Marguerite Henry

Civil War on Sunday, Mary Pope Osborne

Don't Know Much about George Washington, Kenneth C. Davis

Enchanter's Wheel, The, Helen Oakley

George, the Drummer Boy, Nathaniel Benchley

Horses, Horses, Horses, Phyllis R. Fenner

Horse on the Hill, The, Helen Oakley

Misty of Chincoteague, Marguerite Henry

Out of My Shell, Peter Dance

Shell Book, The, Sandra Romashko

Shimmer of Butterflies, A, Joni Phelps Hunt

Horses of Famous Americans

Long before people had cars or buses for transportation, or vehicles, such as tanks or jeeps to take them into battle, the main means of transportation was by horseback. Some horses were used for pulling carriages or wagons and others became famous because they were owned or ridden by generals or presidents.

When the Keswicks purchased the rescue horses, they discovered that they all were named after famous horses, except Sparrow's pony. Here is a little more information about some of the horses named in the book.

Polly Peachum, listed in 1778 as a horse either foaled or purchased by Thomas Jefferson. The "Thomas Jefferson Encyclopedia" also lists horses by the names of Allycrocker, Crab, Orra Moor, Zanga, Brimmer, Bremo and Peacemaker, among the president's many other riding horses.

Liberty, owned by President James Madison, the "father of the Constitution." Madison's home is in Montpelier, Virginia. In 2010, archeological digs at Montpelier focused on locating the structural remains of the stable quarter between the mansion and the visitor center. Dolley Madison's niece, Mary Cutts, wrote that Liberty was well fed and petted in his old age. She claimed, jokingly, that he could open any gate to have his freedom.

Nelson, a sorrel owned by George Washington. He also owned "Blue Skin," a light bluish gray horse. Nelson was his favorite, however. Besides his riding horses, the first president used horses to tread wheat (separating the grain from the stalks) in a sixteen-sided barn at Mount Vernon.

Little Sorrell, a "homely" horse beloved by Confederate General Thomas "Stonewall"

Little Sorrell

Jackson, who was killed during the war. After the war, the horse was displayed at fairs. Southern ladies wove snippets of his tail hair into bracelets.

Old Baldy was ridden by Union General George C. Meade at the Battle of Gettysburg. The horse was wounded several times during

Old Baldy

the Civil War, including at Gettysburg. General Meade mentions this horse in a number of letters during the war, and in one to his wife, on July 7, 1864, he wrote that "I am very much attached to the old brute."

Traveller, owned by Confederate General Robert E. Lee. General Lee bought the gray horse with a long black mane and tail for $200. Traveller was spirited. When the general tried to hold him back when they plunged down a hill, he broke both hands. General Lee's other famous horses were Lucy Long, a sorrel mare, given to him by General J.E.B. Stuart, Richmond and The Roan.

A photograph of General Robert E. Lee, sitting on his favorite horse, Traveller.

Vic and Dandy were favorite horses of General George Armstrong Custer.

Rescue Horses

Bailey and her friends were quite concerned when they saw the condition of the horses that the Keswicks had adopted through a rescue organization. Unfortunately, there are many animals, such as dogs, cats, horses, pigs, birds that are not cared for by their owners and need new homes.

Sometimes the owners move, become ill or lose their jobs and can't afford to care for a pet. Unless they find a new place for the animals to live, the animals may not get enough to eat or the medical care that they need. Some animals die.

Shelter pets and rescue pets especially need good homes.

With the exception of Bailey's kittens, Sallie and Shadow, the cats, dogs and horses in the series were adopted from shelters or through rescue groups.

In Louisa County, Virginia, Weston Farm now has seven rescue horses that arrived with different problems or health conditions.

After several months of good food and care, they are frisky and healthy and enjoy their large grassy pasture at the vineyard.

You can no longer count the ribs on the rescue horses at Weston Farm. Looking over the fence is Deo, one of the newcomers, and below is Charlie, the first horse to arrive at the farm.

Weston Farm rescue horses relax in a pasture.

Dixie, a black and white pinto, is one of the five newest rescue horses at the farm.

Shell Treasures

Sanibel Island, off the Gulf Coast of Florida, is well known for its beautiful shells. Many can easily be found during a beach walk at low tide and others are out beyond the sand bars.

Bailey and her mother found many special shells during their beach walks and she learned about the alphabet cones during a visit to the

Alphabet cone shells displayed at the Bailey-Matthews Shell Museum.

Bailey-Matthews Shell Museum on the Florida island.

According to noted sheller and author Harlan Wittkopf, who wrote a brochure for the museum called *Alphabet Cones: Living, Learning Tools,* shell author Peter Dance was the first person to observe letters and numbers on the alphabet cones (*Conus spurius*).

Wittkopf has been fascinated by the alphabet cones for almost forty years. In 2005 he found two alphabet cone shells that had his initials HEW. He became so interested that he published the brochure, which displays shells with all the letters of the alphabet and numerals through twelve. Children visiting the museum receive copies of the pamphlet.

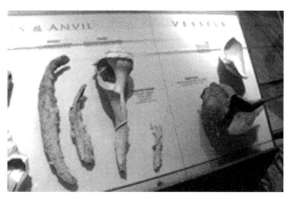

Shell tools on display at the museum.

This exhibit at the Bailey-Matthews Shell Museum depicts the Calusa Indians using shells in everyday life.

Also on display at the Shell Museum are colorful replicas of shell valentines created in the early nineteenth century in the Caribbean for sailors to give to their sweethearts. Pictures taken at museum are used with permission.

Shell Game

What other Sanibel shells are mentioned in this book? Your treasure hunt should take you to titles of book safes and even an author's name.

Hint: Start with cowries, junonias, turkey wings, and olivas.

Bailey's dog is also named for a favorite common shell found on island beaches, but also along the Atlantic coast.

These are just a few of the shells that the author found during early morning walks on one of her favorite Sanibel beaches.

Glossary

currycomb: Used to clean horses' coats, the comb has rows of hard rubber teeth.

ghost light: From a theater superstition. A single bulb left on in a darkened theater stage to keep ghosts away.

groom: To clean a horse or dog's coat.

halter: A rope or strap that goes around a horse's head so the animal can be led.

hieroglyphics: Picture words often found on walls of tombs and sculpture in Egypt.

pinto: A white horse with spots of another color.

sorrel: Light-brown or chestnut colored horse usually with a white mane and tail.

withers: The highest point on the horse's body, not including the neck or head.

mounting block: A box or steps on which to stand on while getting on a horse.

paddock: An enclosed area, like a pen.

Acknowledgments

I am indebted to all who have helped shape, proofread and provide valuable information and fact-checking for this book: My husband Jim; Nancy Miller for her book discussion questions; José Leal, executive director of the Bailey-Matthews Shell Museum, Sanibel; Abbie Grotke; Julie Franklin; Bert and Barbara Stafford; Brenda Anderson of Anderson Farm; Penny Martin, of Weston Farm, Vineyard and Winery; Dr. Lenn Johns; Yvonne Nicholas, and Amber, for inspiration many years ago.

About the Author

 Linda Salisbury draws her inspiration for the Bailey Fish Adventure series from her experiences in Florida and Virginia, and as a mother, grandmother, mentor, and foster mother. She is a musician and enjoys boating and traveling.

Also in the Bailey Fish Adventure series are: *The Wild Women of Lake Anna,* a *ForeWord* magazine finalist for Book of the Year 2005; *No Sisters Sisters Club,* silver finalist in Florida Publishers Association's Best Children's Fiction 2008; *The Thief at Keswick Inn* (winner of the FPA, President's Pick Award 2007); *The Mysterious Jamestown Suitcase* (gold medal for Best Children's Fiction in the 2009 FPA President's Book Awards, a bronze medalist in the Moonbeam Children's Book Awards and *ForeWord* finalist); *Ghost of the Chicken Coop Theater;* and

189

Trouble in Contrary Woods (finalist in the Eric Hoffer awards) and *Captain Calliope and the Great Goateenies.* She's also the author of *Mudd Saves the Earth: Booger Glue, Cow Diapers and Other G̶o̶o̶d̶ Ideas.*

The family cats are either former strays or were in need of a new home.

About the Illustrator

 Illustrator and book designer Carol Tornatore lives in Nokomis, Florida, with her Siamese cats. She has won numerous awards for her innovative book and magazine designs. Some of her other children's books include *Florida A to Z, The Runaway Bed, Zachary Cooks Up Some Fun*, and the *Southern Fossil Discovery* series. She enjoys going to the beach, collecting sea shells, and dancing.